Lonely Girl

Judy Baer

BETHANY HOUSE PUBLISHERS
MINNEAPOLIS, MINNESOTA 55438
A Ministry of Bethany Fellowship, Inc.

Lonely Girl
Judy Baer

Library of Congress Catalog Card Number 92–73063

ISBN 1–55661–280-X

Published by Bethany House Publishers
A Ministry of Bethany Fellowship, Inc.
6820 Auto Club Road, Minneapolis, Minnesota 55438

Printed in the United States of America

Cedar River Daydreams

1 ▪ New Girl in Town
2 ▪ Trouble with a Capital "T"
3 ▪ Jennifer's Secret
4 ▪ Journey to Nowhere
5 ▪ Broken Promises
6 ▪ The Intruder
7 ▪ Silent Tears No More
8 ▪ Fill My Empty Heart
9 ▪ Yesterday's Dream
10 ▪ Tomorrow's Promise
11 ▪ Something Old, Something New
12 ▪ Vanishing Star
13 ▪ No Turning Back
14 ▪ Second Chance
15 ▪ Lost and Found
16 ▪ Unheard Voices
17 ▪ Lonely Girl
18 ▪ More Than Friends

Other Books by Judy Baer

- Paige
- Adrienne
- Dear Judy, What's It Like at Your House?

JUDY BAER received a B.A. in English and Education from Concordia College in Moorhead, Minnesota. She has had over nineteen novels published and is a member of the National Romance Writers of America, the Society of Children's Book Writers and the National Federation of Press Women.

Two of her novels, *Adrienne* and *Paige*, have been prizewinning bestsellers in the Bethany House SPRINGFLOWER SERIES (for girls 12–15). Both books have been awarded first place for juvenile fiction in the National Federation of Press Women's communications contest.

Lonely Girl

“ ‘I was hungry, and you gave me food. I was thirsty, and you gave me something to drink. I was alone and away from home, and you invited me into your house. I was without clothes, and you gave me something to wear. I was sick, and you cared for me. I was in prison, and you visited me.’

“Then the good people will answer, ‘Lord, when did we see you hungry and give you food? When did we see you thirsty and give you something to drink? When did we see you alone and away from home and invite you into our house? When did we see you without clothes and give you something to wear? When did we see you sick or in prison and care for you?’

“Then the King will answer, ‘I tell you the truth. Anything you did for any of my people here, you also did for me.’ ”

Matthew 25:35-40

Chapter One

"Do, re, me-me-me . . ."

"Have you seen my sheet music?"

"Shhh. . . ."

"Quit making so much noise!"

"I'm not making noise. I'm warming up for the next song."

"La, la, la, la, la. . . ."

A boisterous blend of conversation and music filled the air. Several students rearranged their music stands. The tenors grumbled among themselves.

Mrs. Waverly, the choir director, fussed with her sheet music at the front of the room. Her pale beige hair was piled high atop her head and tipped precariously to the left. Three pencils sprouted out of the curls and a fourth rested cozily behind her ear. She frowned as she thumbed through the music looking for a missing score.

"Do you think this practice is ever going to end?" Jennifer Golden whispered to her friend Lexi Leighton.

"I'm beginning to doubt it." Lexi pushed her fingers together and stretched her hands high over her head. "I'm starving to death, aren't you?"

Jennifer clapped her hands over her flat tummy

and whimpered. "By the time I get home, all my mother will see is a skeleton walking through the front door. Do you think we have time to stop somewhere for a pizza? Or . . ." She gave Mrs. Waverly a stern look, ". . . are we going to be here all night?"

Lexi laughed and her face lit, making her look prettier than ever. "I suppose anything is possible. I've never seen Mrs. Waverly so excited about a concert before."

"That's because this is the first Thanksgiving concert the Emerald Tones have given in several years," Jennifer pointed out. "When the Emerald Tones were first organized, it used to be a traditional thing, but for some reason, they stopped doing it. Now Mrs. Waverly wants to resurrect the practice. She's going to have the regular choir sing, too."

"Obviously she wants it to be very special," Lexi commented, "but these endless rehearsals are killers." She caught Todd's gaze from the bass section and gave a little wave.

"I think we can manage 'special' with one-hour rehearsals," Jennifer continued to grumble. "It's after five o'clock and she doesn't give any sign of quitting for the evening."

Lexi dug in the pocket of her jeans and pulled out two pieces of cinnamon gum. They were warm and bent, and the silver foil on the ends was tattered. "Here, have one of these. My brother Ben gave them to me this morning when I left the house."

"Ah, food." Jennifer grabbed for the stick of gum. "At last, nourishment to keep me from fainting away."

"Just don't let it keep you from singing, or Mrs. Waverly will have a fit." Lexi grinned as she peeled the gum and popped it into her mouth. Jennifer didn't exactly look like a skeleton. In fact, she looked extremely healthy with her golden blond hair, ruddy pink cheeks, and Nordic good-looks. Still, Jennifer chawed away on the gum as though she hadn't eaten in a month.

"Tomorrow I'm going to ask Mrs. Waverly if I can bring a snack to practice. Then she can keep us as late as she wants."

Just as Jennifer spoke, Mrs. Waverly tapped her baton on the edge of her music stand. "People. People, may I have your attention?"

The entire chorus turned toward Mrs. Waverly. Though they might be inclined to complain about the long practices, every one of the Emerald Tones liked and respected their director. Mrs. Waverly was one of the best—caring, loving, and firm. Teachers like her didn't come along every day.

"You're going to have to help me, people," Mrs. Waverly pleaded.

"We're singing our best," a weary voice chimed from the front row.

Mrs. Waverly smiled. "I know that. I can *hear* that. What you're going to have to do is help me brainstorm."

"My brain has been denied food too long for that," Jennifer mumbled.

"What about?" Lexi ignored her friend.

"I want this Thanksgiving concert to be particularly meaningful and special."

"We've got great music," someone pointed out.

"And great voices!"

"That's very true," Mrs. Waverly said, her head bobbing in agreement. "But I still feel that something is missing. After all, this is a *thanksgiving* concert. Though I've done my best to choose music that reinforces the theme of giving thanks, I feel that we should do something extra to remind everyone how fortunate we are.

"After all, we do have a lot to be thankful for. Our country, our homes, our families, our schools. Even our friends. It's easy to take things for granted in this day and age. It's also very easy to feel like you're missing something. Television and newspaper ads are always telling us that we need this gadget or that widget, a car, or a new mouthwash. Too often we think about what we *want* rather than about the wonderful things we already *have*."

Lexi could tell by the expression on Mrs. Waverly's face that she was very frustrated.

"I can't think of just the right thing to convey that message." Mrs. Waverly's brow furrowed and her beige hair bobbed. "I'd like a central theme for this concert, one idea on which to hinge the entire performance." She glanced worriedly around the room. "I realize that you're tired now. Perhaps this isn't the best time to ask for your help."

There were nods of agreement throughout the room.

"However, I'd like you to help me think of ideas to make this concert the most meaningful ever. Would you do that for me?"

"You bet."

"Sure."

"Why not?"

"Anything to get out of here."

"Tomorrow I want all of you to come back with ideas for a central theme that will make our concert the most meaningful Thanksgiving concert Cedar River has ever had. You're dismissed."

The students pressed eagerly toward the door.

"Why is she so persistent about this 'best and most meaningful Thanksgiving concert ever'?" Jennifer muttered as she pushed forward in the crowd. "Why can't we just get up and sing like always?"

"I think I understand," Lexi said. "Thanksgiving is the kind of holiday that needs some extra thought. It's one time in the year when we should think about the good things we have and not complain about the things we don't have. Mrs. Waverly wants to get that point across. She wants us to feel grateful, not selfish."

"That's easy for you, Lexi," Jennifer said dourly. "You're always sunny, happy, and cheerful. Me—I'm different. Crabby. Grouchy. A real scrooge."

"Oh, you are not." Lexi poked her friend in the ribs. "You're just hungry."

"Maybe that's it." Jennifer nodded. "I'm always grouchy when I'm hungry. I guess that means I'll have to eat a big supper before the Thanksgiving concert, huh?"

They spilled into the hallway like water from a faucet, everyone heading for their lockers. Lexi grabbed two of her textbooks and slammed her locker door. As she turned, Todd Winston was at her side.

"I've got the Bomb today, Lexi. Do you need a ride home?"

"Of course," Lexi agreed eagerly.

"Can I have a ride, too?" Jennifer piped. "I'm practically fainting from hunger."

Todd looked her over from head to toe. His handsome face split in a wide grin. "Why, Jennifer, I didn't even see you there! Have you been dieting? You look so thin, you've practically disappeared."

"Very funny," Jennifer retorted. "Sarcasm will get you nowhere, Todd. For that, you have to drive me home first."

"Good idea, Golden. That means I'll get you out of the car as fast as possible."

The playful banter continued as the three walked to the parking lot. Lexi crawled into the front seat of the old blue '49 Ford Coupe as Jennifer scrambled into the backseat.

Todd, an antique car buff, patted the hood of his pride and joy. "It sure feels good to be driving again," he commented.

"It sure feels good to be *riding* again," Jennifer retorted. "I was sick of walking back and forth to and from school. It's much more fun bumming rides from you."

Todd had been unable to drive while he was recovering from a football injury that had threatened to leave him paralyzed. Now that he was well again, his doctors had recently given him the go-ahead to resume a normal schedule.

That is one thing we can all be thankful for this Thanksgiving, Lexi mused as she listened with half an ear to Todd and Jennifer's conversation. She leaned her head against the soft, velvety car seat and gazed through half-closed lids at the already empty school. She was startled to see a lone, obscure figure dart out of a side doorway. The figure hovered for a moment in the shadows before sprinting off into the deepening dusk.

How strange. Who would be hanging around the school at this hour? Only the Emerald Tones were practicing this late. No one else rehearsed in this wing of the school building.

What's more, the Emerald Tones always left through the main door by the lockers. The side door was rarely used by students. Lexi was mildly curious about who might be furtively sneaking out of the school, but when Todd threw his arm around Lexi's shoulder and gave her a squeeze, she forgot all about the disappearing shadow.

"You're up early," Mrs. Leighton greeted Lexi as she bolted into the kitchen.

Lexi grabbed a glass from the table and splashed it full of freshly squeezed orange juice. "I want to be at school as soon as the doors open this morning." Lexi edged one arm into her jacket while feeding herself a piece of cinnamon toast with the other hand. "These extra rehearsals for the Emerald Tones have kept me so busy that I haven't had time to finish my photo captions for the next edition of the *Cedar River Review.* If I get there early, I can finish the captions and turn them in before my first class." She gulped down another glass of orange juice. "You don't mind, do you, if I don't sit down with you this morning?"

"I'm getting used to it, Lexi. You certainly are busy these days."

Lexi leaned over and gave her mother a kiss. "As soon as this concert is over, I'll turn into a civilized person again. I promise."

"What's a *cibilized* person?" Benjamin Leighton wondered as he stumbled downstairs for his breakfast.

"Civilized, Benjamin, not *cibilized*," Lexi corrected with a laugh. "It means I'll start being a lady again and sit down at the breakfast table and have breakfast with you instead of running off."

"Oh." Ben vigorously rubbed his dark eyes. His hair stood in spiky points atop his head. He curled and uncurled his toes as if willing them to wake up. "I don't want to be *cibilized* today, either. I want to go back to bed."

"You can't, Ben. They'll miss you at the Academy."

Ben, who was born with Down's syndrome, went to a special school for children like him.

"School won't be any fun for your friends if you're not there," Lexi coaxed.

Benjamin thought about that for a moment. "It's fun when I'm there," he agreed. He gave a huge, cheek-stretching yawn. "I guess I'd better go to school."

"Atta boy, Ben." Lexi tousled his hair. "Now I'd better get going, too."

"Do you want a ride?" Mrs. Leighton asked. "Your father is tinkering with the car. Maybe you can still catch him."

"Good idea." Lexi bolted through the door and into the garage. Her father was just slipping behind the wheel.

"Are you ready to go, Lexi?" he asked.

"Sure." Lexi gave her father a big smile. Lexi was very proud of her veterinarian dad. Dr. Leighton looked particularly handsome today in a navy blue blazer, white shirt, and red and blue tie. "You're all dressed up," Lexi noted. "You must not have any surgery this morning."

"Actually, I have a meeting at the bank before I go to the clinic."

"I appreciate the ride." Lexi sat back and inhaled the fresh, crisp air. "I have lots to do before my first class."

"I'm glad to have you. We've both been so busy lately we haven't had time for a good conversation." Her father smiled at her. His was a smile many people said reminded them of Lexi—wide, open, and appealing.

"I noticed that Todd dropped you off last night. It's good to see him behind the wheel of a car again."

Lexi nodded enthusiastically. "He's so much stronger and steadier now than he was. It's practically a miracle."

"Well, they do happen," Dr. Leighton said with conviction. "We all know that. By the way, how's that new friend of yours? The one whose parents are missionaries?"

"You mean Ruth. She's fine. She still hasn't heard when she's to go and live with her parents, so she's assuming that she'll be in Cedar River for the entire school year."

"Is she happy about that?"

"Yes and no. She'd like to be with her parents, but she's made some really good friends here. I guess because of her hearing impairment, that hasn't always happened in other schools she's attended. I think Ruth will be sad to leave Cedar River."

"I hope it works out for the best." Lexi's father smiled. "You've made some pretty good friends yourself, haven't you, Lexi?"

"The best. I don't know what I'd do without Egg and Binky, Jennifer, Peggy, Todd, and Anna Marie.

And then there's Matt and Harry and . . ." Lexi paused.

She'd almost added Minda to her list of friends. But she and Minda were really more like friendly enemies. They didn't get along too well, yet they'd been there for each other during crises. If Minda weren't a member of the elite social clique, the Hi-Fives, Lexi thought they might have had a better chance of becoming friends.

Dr. Leighton didn't give Lexi much time to think about her problems with Minda. "Any chance you're going to be free to help me at the veterinary clinic one of these days?" he asked. "I need the cages hosed out and I've got a whole list of other chores for you to do."

Lexi winced. "I don't know, Dad. I'll try to come in after school, but I can't make any promises. I've been really busy. Not only have I been doing pictures for the school paper and taking a heavy class load, but Mrs. Waverly has really been piling on the extra rehearsals for the Emerald Tones. I can probably help you once the concert is over."

"Well, see what you can do," Dr. Leighton said. He pulled into the driveway of the school. "You're early, Lexi. Looks like you've arrived before most of the teachers today."

"That's all right. The janitors come at daybreak. I see lights on inside the building."

"I've never seen a student so anxious to get to school in the morning."

"Believe me, if I didn't have those captions to do, I wouldn't be here. Tim Anders and Egg McNaughton have both been nagging at me to get them done. I promised they'd be in the *Review* room before school today."

"I'm glad to see you're keeping your promises." Dr. Leighton leaned over and gave his daughter a kiss on the cheek. "Have a good day, Lexi."

"Bye, Dad. Thanks." She slammed the car door and moved toward the wide double doors at the school's entrance. Silence surrounded her like a blanket as she stepped into the school building. *I've never seen it this quiet before*, Lexi thought as she moved toward her locker. The halls seemed wider and higher without students crowding them.

Lexi took her jacket and books to her locker and retrieved a pencil. *If I hurry, I can have those captions done in no time*, she told herself. Maybe there'd even be a few minutes to get a head start on reviewing for her first-hour class.

On the way to the *Cedar River Review* room, Lexi took a detour to the girls' rest room. As she opened the first of the two doors, she was surprised to hear the splash of running water. *Who could be here this early?* Then an answer occurred to her: a janitor, of course.

Funny, she thought the janitors usually propped the doors open when they cleaned the rest rooms. Without any more thought about it, Lexi pushed the door open and walked inside. Much to her surprise, Lexi saw a slender girl in faded jeans and a soft white T-shirt washing her face and hands at the sink.

The girl's hair was slightly tousled, as though she'd been up only a few minutes. On the rim of the sink she balanced a shabby clear plastic travel bag with foundation makeup, an eyeliner stick, and a tube of mascara. Beside the makeup bag was a toothbrush and a tube of toothpaste. It appeared the dark-eyed girl was getting ready for school right here in the girls' rest room.

Startled by the intrusion, the girl looked up, her cheeks still damp, challenge in her eyes. *Go ahead, ask me what I'm doing here. I dare you. But you'll regret it,* her look seemed to say.

Before Lexi could gather her thoughts to speak, the girl pushed the rest of her belongings into the bag and brushed past her without a word, leaving Lexi alone in the rest room with the slow drip of the faucet.

Lexi stared at herself in the mirror. Her eyes looker bigger than usual, and her cheeks were pale. She felt a twinge of guilt for having apparently scared the poor girl out of the rest room. But what was she doing in here at this hour of the morning?

It looked as if she was getting ready for school, but how could that be? Why would anyone get ready here instead of in the privacy of their own home, unless they were late; and that certainly wasn't the case. Lexi stared at the sink. Soap bubbles made a fragile wreath around the drain. There were flecks of pink blusher and a drop of black mascara against the whiteness of the porcelain bowl.

Lexi dismissed the feeling that this was a strange encounter. Cedar River was a large school. Perhaps there were more early-morning activities going on than she'd realized. Lexi dug into her pocket and pulled out a comb. After a quick touch up on her hair, she headed for the *Review* workroom.

It was a long morning for Lexi. She was yawning by the time the lunch bell rang. She met Ruth Nelson in the hallway on the way to the lunchroom. Ruth wore a wide smile and her eyes sparkled with pleasure.

"Hi, Lexi. How are you today?"

"Just fine. How are you?"

"I couldn't be better."

As they entered the lunchroom, they saw Todd, Egg and Binky McNaughton, Jennifer, Peggy, Matt Windsor, and Anna Marie Arnold.

"Looks like everyone's already been through the line," Ruth said, humming a little tune under her breath as she picked up silverware from the round canisters, and took a tray from the stack. Ruth began to hum louder as she pushed past the cafeteria food display and made her selections.

"What are you so happy about today?" Lexi asked, taking an ice cream cup from the bin. "You act like you just received some good news."

"Actually, I did." Ruth gave her a silly smile. "It's great news to me, anyway."

"What is it?"

"I'm happy because I'm not the newest girl in school anymore." Ruth rolled her eyes. "Finally 'the new girl and her hearing aids' will be old news around Cedar River. I can't tell you how relieved I am. Maybe now that there's another newcomer in school, people will quit asking questions and treat me like a normal student."

"New girl? I didn't realize there was a new girl in school." By this time, Lexi and Ruth had reached the table where their friends had congregated.

Egg looked up from a plate of ham and creamed corn. "There's a new girl at school? I didn't know that. When did she come?"

"Are you sure?" Jennifer said with a slight frown.

"I usually hear about everything in study hall. I didn't hear anything about a new girl."

"Maybe you're mistaken, Ruth," Binky offered. "I remember when you came. We all knew about you in a matter of minutes." Binky's expression turned impish. "It was the same way when Lexi moved to town. New girls certainly know how to be the center of attention."

"Well this girl must not," Ruth said firmly, "because she's in school and she's new. She's right over there." Ruth pointed to a girl at the far end of the room. "See her? She's the one sitting alone in faded jeans and a men's T-shirt."

Lexi's mouth dropped open. It was the girl she'd seen in the rest room earlier that morning. Her shoulder-length hair was dark and shiny. It looked clean, but was poorly cut, the bangs too long and falling into her eyes. She had pale white skin, almost as white as her T-shirt, and a small nose that turned up. She may have even been pretty if she didn't look so tense and unhappy.

"She's cute," Binky said.

"But she looks awfully serious and she's not very well dressed," Anna Marie added.

Anna Marie rarely said anything critical about anyone, but Lexi tended to agree with her friend. She'd noticed earlier that the new girl's jeans were worn and stained, not "designer-worn," with intentional cuts and ragged edges, but just plain old. Her oversized T-shirt also looked worn out, and she wore a man's leather belt and plain tennis shoes—not exactly the wardrobe Lexi would have chosen for her first day at a new school.

"Do you think one of us should go over and say

hello to her?" Binky asked.

"I tried to smile at her when she went by," Peggy said, "but she wouldn't look at me. She stared straight ahead like she didn't want to catch anyone's eye."

"Let's give her a day or two to get used to us before we all jump down her neck," Jennifer suggested. "After all, I think we just about scared Ruth to death when she moved to Cedar River."

Ruth laughed brightly. "I didn't know what to think of all of you," she admitted. "And I was worried about how you would accept my hearing handicap. Now I know I had nothing to worry about. We'll have to let this new girl know she's okay, and we accept her."

"Matt and I will leave that up to you girls," Todd said with a grin. "I suppose if we were too friendly to all the new girls in school, we'd get in trouble with the *old* ones."

"Good idea, Winston," Jennifer said, patting him on the shoulder. "Lexi and I wouldn't like it if you got too friendly with every new girl—Egg, what's wrong with you?" Jennifer asked.

Egg McNaughton sat transfixed, his eyes staring straight ahead. "Huh?" Egg said dully. His gaze never flickered. His eyes were glued to the new girl across the room.

"Egg? Hello in there. Are you all right?" Binky almost shouted at her brother.

Now everyone was staring at him.

Lexi waved a hand in front of his eyes, but he didn't even flinch. "Why are you staring, Egg?" She put her hand on his arm and gave him a slight shake. He looked away and blinked as if he were waking from a dream.

"I was . . . I was looking at the new girl," he said, his voice betraying his interest.

"So? Big deal. We were, too. But none of us have that goofy, dreamy look on our face." Binky could always be counted on to be blunt where her brother was concerned.

"But don't you see?" Egg asked, a wondering tone in his voice.

"See what?" Jennifer asked.

"How beautiful she is," Egg's voice lowered reverently. "She's a real knockout. I know her clothes aren't so neat, but she has a great face, and gorgeous hair!" Egg enthused.

She *was* pretty, but listening to Egg you'd think a glamorous movie star had just graced the Cedar River High cafeteria.

"Oh-oh," Lexi muttered to Todd. "I think we're in trouble."

Todd glanced at Egg, who was still staring across the room with a love-sick gaze.

"Last time he looked that way, he was crazy about Minda Hannaford," Lexi reminded Todd. "Don't you remember?"

Todd gave a soft groan. "You don't think Egg's falling in love again, do you?"

"I'd guarantee it. Look at that expression on his face."

Egg looked as happy and sappy as a kitten who'd just filled his stomach with pure cream.

"If cupid's arrow has hit Egg again, that means disaster is about to strike," Todd announced to no one in particular.

Egg was an all-or-nothing kind of guy. He was either totally in love and actively pursuing a girl from morning to night, or he wasn't interested at all. Lexi hoped for Egg's own sake that the silly calf-like look on his face would pass quickly.

Just then, she felt Todd's elbow graze her ribs. "Look, here comes Minda," he whispered. "Let's see what happens."

Minda Hannaford, dressed as usual in the latest fashion, strutted by their table and tossed a saucy look their way. Minda had known perfectly well how crazy Egg was about her and had managed to ignore him anyway. The harder Egg had pursued her, the less likely Minda had been to pay attention to him. Still, she couldn't help but tease Egg once in awhile with one of her coy smiles.

Her smile today, however, seemed to bounce off Egg like a rubber ball. She passed right in front of him, but Egg acted as though he didn't even know Minda was there.

Minda blinked twice and with an indignant little huff, stomped off.

"It's trouble. I can see it coming. T-r-o-u-b-l-e."

"What do you mean?" Binky asked, getting worried.

Todd nodded toward Egg. "Does anyone believe in love at first sight?"

Peggy and Jennifer groaned together. "Oh, no. You don't mean Egg and . . ."

"Egg, don't fall in love with her. You don't even know who she is. Egg? Egg . . ." Binky collapsed against the back of her chair with a defeated groan.

Then with a sharpness that made them all jump, the warning bell rang.

"Time to go," Matt Windsor muttered. "Do you think Egg can pry his eyes loose?"

No one answered. Instead they all watched Egg scramble from his seat, pack his afternoon books under his arm and hurry through the doorway after the new girl.

"I can't believe it," Jennifer groaned. "The weirdness is going to start all over again."

"When is my brother ever going to learn?" Binky moaned. "He falls in and out of love like other people dive in and out of swimming pools!"

"All I can tell you, Binky, is this," Jennifer said with a firm note in her voice. "If your brother Egg is going to fall head-over-heels-in-love with the girl, I think we'd better find out who she is!"

Chapter Two

"Come on." Jennifer gestured to the other three girls and headed for the hall. "Let's follow her."

Lexi was relieved to see that the new girl had disappeared in the throng of students.

"Where did she go?" Jennifer stomped her foot impatiently and stared down the hallway.

"It was as though she knew we wanted to talk to her and she ran away," Binky complained.

"Aren't you guys carrying this a little too far?" Lexi asked her friends.

"If you want to find out more about the new girl, why don't you try to get to know her as a friend?" Peggy added.

"I suppose you two are right."

"We just know how Egg acts when he thinks he's in love."

"She'd better be nice," Binky said, her eyes narrowing. "I don't want my brother's feelings hurt again."

Lexi threw her hands in the air. "Give the poor girl a break! She hasn't done a thing."

"She's right," Binky said to Jennifer. "Egg's the one who's acting goofy."

"Just the same," Jennifer retorted with a determined expression on her face, "I'd like to find out exactly who this new girl is."

Jennifer, Peggy, Binky, and Lexi discovered that getting information about the new girl was easier said than done. The girl was quiet in class, never asking or answering a question unless a teacher called on her. Her homework was always done, and she never caused any problems that might call attention to herself.

As the gang discovered during that week, Angela Hardy was unwilling to talk to anyone in the hallways. She kept her head down, her eyes focused on the tiled floor. What's more, she regularly slipped out of the school immediately after the final bell. Though both Jennifer and Binky tried several times to catch her, they never succeeded.

"She vanishes into thin air!" Binky complained. "How can we ever get to know a girl who acts like that?"

Lexi didn't have an answer for her friend, and her own questions about the new girl were beginning to multiply.

"Do you want to go to the mall?" Jennifer asked when Lexi came to the door. Peggy and Binky stood with Jennifer on Lexi's front steps Saturday morning. They wore jackets, and their purses were slung casually over their shoulders.

"We haven't gone shopping together in a long time," Binky reminded Lexi.

"Sure, why not? Mom and Ben just went to the

grocery store. Hang on. I'll leave them a note."

"The parking lot looks empty today," Peggy commented once they reached the mall. "I wonder where everyone is?"

"I'm glad it's empty." Binky clambered down the bus steps and hurried toward the entrance. "We can shop more freely that way. I'm looking for a pair of earrings to match my new blouse. They have to be absolutely perfect because I only have money for one pair."

Peggy, Lexi, and Jennifer groaned in unison. They were fully aware of Binky's financial situation. Whenever Binky got extra money and decided she needed something to be "perfect," she could waste an entire day before settling on a purchase.

"Binky, do you have to shop for earrings in every store in the mall?" Jennifer complained. "My feet hurt."

Binky slowed her step. "Sorry, guys. Have I been wearing you out?"

"I feel like I've been competing in a triathalon," Lexi admitted. "Speed-walking, hurdle-jumping, and power-shopping. What's with you today anyway, Binky?"

Binky sat down on a bench in the center of the mall, put her hands to her forehead and groaned. "Even shopping doesn't make me feel any better," she wailed.

Peggy and Lexi exchanged worried glances. This was hardly what they had expected from their fun-loving friend!

"What's wrong, Bink?" Lexi put a hand on Binky's thin shoulder.

Binky looked up and gave Lexi a weak smile. "It's silly, really. Just plain stupid. I don't know why I'm acting this way. I'm just so disgusted with my brother."

"*Egg* is the one who's got you so upset today?" Peggy interjected. "Why? What did he do?"

"He's driving me crazy."

"What's new about that?" Jennifer pointed out. "Egg always drives you crazy, and vice versa."

"Oh, it's not the normal irritating stuff that's getting me down," Binky assured Jennifer. "It's the weird stuff he's been doing lately that has to do with . . . with *that girl*!"

"Ohhh . . . Angela Hardy." Jennifer guessed.

Binky nodded her head vigorously. "Egg's still moping around the house like a love-sick puppy."

"Well, I was right. Egg *is* in love again." Lexi still hadn't forgotten the silly things Egg had once done to capture Minda Hannaford's attention—like taking steroids to "bulk up." When Egg thought he was in love, his common sense flew out the window.

"What's scary is that he's getting worse every day. This morning I caught him spelling 'Angela' with his alphabet cereal. He'd eaten all the other letters and was trying to make A-N-G-E-L-A float in the milk in a straight line."

Peggy giggled. "Leave it to Egg to think of something creative."

"It's not funny, Peggy." Binky was indignant. "He's scribbled her name all over his notebook covers, and drawn hearts and wedding bells in the margins of every page."

"Yuck!" Jennifer made a face. "He must be crazy."

"That's my point exactly," Binky wailed. "Egg never does anything halfway. He's either in love or he's out of it."

"But what about his friendships with Anna Marie and Ruth?" Jennifer asked. "He's never been that way with either of them."

"I think Egg has a screw loose in his brain," Binky said morosely. "He's not rowing with both oars in the water. He's not playing Monopoly with both dice. He's not . . ."

"We get the idea, Binky. You think Egg's gone crazy over Angela and you don't know what to do about it."

"Right. He tries every day to talk to her and she completely ignores him."

"I think Egg likes the challenge. The harder a girl is to get to know, and the more uninterested she seems, the more he likes her."

"Well, he shouldn't feel badly that she's treating him that way," Jennifer pointed out. "She'll hardly talk to any of us."

Lexi, too, had tried on many occasions to start a conversation, but Angela seemed determined to answer only yes or no.

"She's really secretive," Jennifer continued. "When I asked her where she came from and where she lives now, she gave a funny little smile and shrugged. She wouldn't answer me. Don't you think that's weird?"

"Maybe she thinks it's none of your business," Peggy guessed.

"Why should it be a secret?" Jennifer retorted. "We all know she has to live *somewhere* in Cedar

River. It would certainly help if she were just a little more friendly."

"Maybe she's shy," Peggy suggested. "After all, Ruth was hard to get to know at first. Now she's as friendly a person as you'll ever meet."

"I don't think Angela's the least bit like Ruth," Binky insisted. "Ruth had a reason to be shy. With those big hearing aids in her ears, she was bound to feel self-conscious."

"Maybe Angela feels self-conscious about something else."

"I can't imagine what it could be," Binky muttered. "She's pretty and she's smart."

"How do you know she's smart?" Jennifer inquired. "She never opens her mouth in class."

"I know, but I've seen the grades on her papers when the teacher hands them back. I've even seen some A+'s."

Jennifer whistled. "Wow, I'd like to pull a few A+'s myself. If I were getting those kind of grades, I'd be smiling and talking to everyone."

"You always *do* smile and talk to everyone," Peggy pointed out.

"I suppose that's true," Jennifer admitted. "Angela acts like she doesn't want to get close to anyone—ever."

The four girls left the bench and made their way to the yogurt stand. Binky dug out some coins and bought a vanilla cone. After licking the curl on top thoughtfully, she announced, "I'll bet I know what's wrong with Angela."

"Okay, Sherlock Holmes, why doesn't Angela want to get close to anyone?" Peggy asked.

"I think she's keeping a secret. A big secret. Maybe even a *bad* secret."

"Oh, Binky, get real. What kind of a secret would Angela have? She's just a kid!" Jennifer said.

"Kids have secrets sometimes," Lexi said knowingly. Then she turned an appraising eye on Binky. "What if Angela is just terribly shy? Maybe we've all scared her away by being *too* friendly. Maybe what Angela needs is time to get used to living here in Cedar River, to get used to us."

"I don't think so, Lexi," Jennifer disagreed. "The more I think about it, the more I think Binky's right. Angela is mysterious. She never talks to anyone. She never stays around school after the bell rings, and she refuses to take part in any school activities. There's definitely some mystery in her life she's trying to hide."

"Oh, Jennifer," Peggy said, laughing. "You have an overactive imagination. You've been reading too many mystery novels from the library."

Jennifer shook her head somberly. "No, I don't think so. Angela's not like any other teenage girl I've ever known. One, she never fusses with her hair or clothes. She *always* wears jeans and a T-shirt. Two, she avoids the boys especially, and three, she doesn't smile—even when she gets A+ on a paper! Has anyone *ever* seen Angela smile?"

"I guess not," Lexi admitted.

"You've seen her bolt from her desk at the end of the day. She's down the hall and out the door before the rest of us have reached our lockers. It's like she's afraid one of us will suggest we walk home together."

"Maybe she has an after-school job or something," Binky suggested.

"That could explain it, I suppose," Jennifer said doubtfully. "But why is she always at school so early in the morning? She's always the first one in the classroom. Have you noticed that?"

"What does that have to do with anything?" Lexi asked, although she still remembered the morning she'd run into Angela putting makeup on in the girls' rest room.

"If she's got an after-school job, don't you think she'd take her time in the morning? Why would she hurry to sit in an empty classroom?"

"Ooohhh, maybe you're right." Binky's eyes grew round and worried-looking.

It was hard for Lexi to find reasons to disagree with Jennifer. Angela Hardy was a very strange girl. Still, Lexi didn't like her friends' overactive imaginations working to conjure up "what-if" scenarios for Angela's life.

A small whimper escaped Binky's lips as she dropped the half-eaten yogurt cone into a waste can. "This is awful!" she exclaimed.

"Was something wrong with your cone?" Jennifer asked.

"No, no. It's Angela. Angela and Egg. Don't you see? I feel worse than ever now. My brother has a terrible crush on someone who has some horrible mystery about her," Binky moaned. "Poor Egg is going to have his heart broken again. He's going to be hurt. I just know it."

"You're overreacting, Binky," Peggy assured her. "Egg can take care of himself."

Binky shook her head. "You can't say that about Egg, Peggy. Especially not where his love life is concerned. You know how batty he went over Minda."

"But Egg learned his lesson, didn't he?"

"I don't think so." Binky's expression grew more

pained. "I'll tell you guys a secret if you promise, absolutely promise with your life, that you won't tell anyone."

"Of course we promise," Jennifer said. "We're friends. We don't tell on each other."

Binky's shoulders drooped. "Egg admitted to me that he's tried to follow Angela home three or four times."

"You're kidding!" Lexi gasped.

"I know. It sounds wild, but Egg tried to follow her home. He had this idea that if he could talk to her in private and tell her about himself, she'd warm up to him."

"He *is* crazy." Jennifer shook her head. "What happened?"

"Egg said that every time he followed her, he'd lose her."

"How could he lose her?" Jennifer wondered. "Angela's new in town. Egg has lived here all his life!"

"Egg says she takes a different route home from school every night."

"That's weird," Peggy said.

"I know. That's what Egg thought. He said it's always a complicated route, and she dodges in and out of buildings. He could never figure out where she was going. Every time he tried to follow her, she managed to ditch him. It was as though she were *expecting* someone to follow her. He said she walked quickly, looking over her shoulder every now and then. She seemed worried that someone would see where she was going."

"Didn't Egg get the idea that perhaps she didn't *want* anyone following her?" Lexi asked softly.

"You know Egg, once he gets an idea in his head,

it's stuck there forever. Besides, Egg thought he was doing a good job of following her, staying out of sight most of the time. Still, she acted like an escaped convict or something."

"This is too much. This is just too much." Jennifer began pacing the floor, clenching and unclenching her fists. "Something is going on. I can feel it in my bones. No normal person acts like that on their way home from school. Angela Hardy has something to hide."

It was apparent that Jennifer's sleuthing instincts were taking over. Lexi felt a sinking sensation in the pit of her stomach. First Egg, now Jennifer—*poor Angela*!

"So, you all agree there's something mysterious about Angela?" Binky asked, looking to her friends for help.

"I don't think so, I *know* so," Jennifer insisted. "She's acting *very* strangely. Egg would never mention the fact that he'd followed her home if she'd walk home like a normal person."

"I guess not." Binky looked confused. "But even if she is acting mysteriously, what can *we* do about it?"

"I'm going to follow Angela home myself," Jennifer announced, squaring her shoulders. "It's obvious that this is something Egg can't handle on his own. He's going to need some help from me."

"Jennifer, don't be silly."

"I'm not being silly, Peggy. This is weird and I want to get to the bottom of it."

"I don't think it's a good idea, either," Lexi added. "Angela Hardy seems like a very shy, quiet person. For one of my friends to be following her home seems kind of . . . creepy."

"She's the one who's creepy, Lexi." Jennifer thrust her chin out determinedly. The more Lexi tried to talk her out of it, the more insistent Jennifer seemed to become.

"Jennifer," Lexi said matter-of-factly, "if Angela wanted people to know where she lived, she'd tell them. How would you feel if someone started to follow you home at night?"

"I don't have anything to hide," Jennifer retorted. "I might think it a little crazy or weird if Egg followed me home, but I'd probably be flattered if someone were that interested in me."

"You'd think it was creepy, Jennifer, you know you would," Lexi insisted.

"You guys aren't talking me out of this one," Jennifer said. "Egg has a crush on a very strange and mysterious girl, and I think it's up to some of his friends to find out exactly what's going on with her."

As if to change the subject, Jennifer marched off to stand in front of a store display window. "Look at those boots! Aren't they great?"

"They look like combat boots to me," Binky said.

"I know. Don't you just love them? Come on. Let's go inside and take a look." Jennifer grabbed Binky and Lexi by the wrists and towed them into the store, with Peggy close behind.

When they emerged, they ran into Minda Hannaford and Tressa and Gina Williams staring at the same pair of boots in the window.

"How do you like them?" Jennifer asked jauntily.

"I love them," Minda said, dreamy-eyed.

"I wonder if they have my size," Tressa added.

"Do they have them in other colors?" Gina wondered aloud.

"Forget it girls—they're mine," Jennifer announced proudly. "I just put a pair on layaway."

Minda made a face and stomped her foot. "I was going to buy those, Jennifer Golden. They're just what I wanted."

"Too late, they're mine now, Minda. You wouldn't want to wear a pair of boots that *I* owned first."

Minda's eyes narrowed. "If I paid cash for them, I could take mine home. You've got yours on layaway."

"That's not fair!" Jennifer protested.

Minda laughed mockingly. "Don't worry about it, Golden. I wouldn't dream of buying those boots if you're going to wear them. I like to own *one-of-a-kind* clothing. I want people to copy *my* fashions."

"I knew I could count on you, Minda." Jennifer grinned.

"What are you guys up to?" Tressa asked Lexi.

"Just looking around. Binky's looking for earrings, and she has to look in every store first."

"Yeah, Gina does, too." Tressa snapped her gum. "You know, I'm kind of hungry. Does anyone feel like an Orange Julius and some fries?"

"Gross! They're both terrible for the figure and the complexion," Minda said.

"Sounds good to me," Binky said. "I'll have some with you, Tressa."

Tressa blinked. It was not often the Hi-Fives associated with nonmembers of their club. She thought for a minute and then shrugged. "Okay, come on. Let's go."

"How about a bag of yogurt-covered raisins," Binky suggested, distracted by a display of them. "I just *love* yogurt-covered raisins."

After grabbing their snacks, the girls walked through the mall, munching on fries and raisins and slurping on Orange Julius', all the while critiquing the clothing in store windows. Next, they tried perfume testers at a cosmetics counter, and helped Binky pick out a pair of huge hoop earrings that grazed her shoulders when she walked.

It was just after five when Minda announced, "I have to go home. My dad's taking me out for dinner tonight and I have to get ready." She turned to Lexi, Jennifer, Peggy, and Binky. "Did you drive over here?" she asked.

"No, we took the bus," Binky blurted.

"I can give you a ride home if you'd like."

The girls tried not to show their surprise.

"That would be great, Minda. Thanks," Lexi said.

Minda dropped the girls off on a street corner between Binky's house and Lexi's. The four clambered out of the car, thanking Minda again for the ride.

When Minda had driven off, Jennifer whistled through her teeth. "That's a stretch. Minda was actually nice today. Well, I've gotta go. See you all later." Jennifer sauntered off with a wave.

"Yeah, I'm taking off, too," Peggy said. "You coming, Binky?"

"Sure. It's my turn to set the table for supper tonight. "Bye, Lexi." Binky and Peggy took off in the other direction.

Lexi watched her friends walk away and breathed a sigh of relief. For once she was grateful to Minda for the distraction. Jennifer hadn't said another word about following Angela home from school. *Oh, please,* Lexi thought, *let Jennifer forget all about what she said!*

The Emerald Tones' rehearsal was over, but the discussion about the upcoming Thanksgiving concert was still in full swing. Mrs. Waverly's voice carried over the chatter of the students.

"Did everyone understand? I want each of you to bring canned goods or money to the concert. We will then make up Thanksgiving food baskets for the poor of our city. You can bring canned vegetables, cranberry sauce, stuffing mix, sweet potatoes. The corner grocer will give us a special discount on turkeys, so if you bring money, you can be assured it will be spent to buy turkey and potatoes for the baskets."

"Are we going to buy actual baskets to hold the food?" someone asked.

"No. Let's spend our money for the food itself. The baskets can be simple grocery boxes. We can decorate them with a ribbon, a card, maybe some colored foil. I'll leave that up to you students. I want each of you to experience the joy of giving to someone less fortunate."

"You really are excited about this, aren't you, Mrs. Waverly?" one of the boys in the front row asked.

Mrs. Waverly nodded so energetically, a yellow pencil flew out of the curls in her hair. "It's something that's been important to me for a long time. During this past year I've finally taken the time to do volunteer work at the local mission. I must say it's changed my life."

Tim Anders gave a little shudder. "What's it like down there anyway? Pretty bad?"

Mrs. Waverly shook her head. "Not at all. The

mission is a very pleasant place. It's very clean, for one thing. And there are lots of big windows to let in the sunshine. But the most special thing about the mission is the people who work there. I've learned so much from them these past weeks. They are deeply sensitive to the needs of the poor and the homeless."

Tressa gave a loud unladylike snort at the word *homeless*. Several choir members turned to stare at her.

Mrs. Waverly's eyebrows arched so high they nearly disappeared beneath her hair. "Tressa!"

"Sorry, Mrs. Waverly, but I just couldn't help it. You said the people at the mission were sensitive to the needs of the poor and homeless. Well, I don't think there *are* any homeless in Cedar River. It can't be a very hard job to be sensitive to people who don't even exist."

"What makes you think there are no homeless people in Cedar River, Tressa?"

"I would have seen them. We go downtown all the time—down by the train station, and all those scummy older apartment buildings. There aren't any homeless people around there. I've never seen bag ladies or people sleeping on grates, either. I think the people at the mission are feeding you a line, Mrs. Waverly. There aren't any homeless in Cedar River."

"I have to disagree with you, Tressa. There are homeless people *everywhere*. Even here in Cedar River. I have seen them. In fact, there are several homeless people living at the mission right now."

Tressa shook her head in disbelief. She folded her arms across her chest and wore her trademark stubborn look. "Maybe, Mrs. Waverly, if you say so. If you've seen them at the mission, I guess I can't argue with that. Still, I don't think the homeless have such a bad deal, anyway."

"Oh?" Mrs. Waverly's expression was one of shock.

"Just think about it. The people you're talking about are eating three square meals a day, with a roof over their heads—and they're not paying a dime for it!"

Tressa was just getting warmed up. "My dad says he's getting tired of paying taxes for people who don't pay their own way. He says the people we call homeless today used to be called *bums*. My dad is a hard-working, honest taxpayer, who'd like to see his money go for things that benefit *him*, instead of people who are too lazy to make it in life."

"Most of the homeless would like to pay their way, Tressa, but circumstances prevent them from doing so."

"Circumstances? Ha!"

Lexi could tell by Tressa's enthusiasm that this particular topic of conversation had been discussed more than once at the Williams' home.

"My dad says homeless people are homeless by choice. They're just too lazy to work."

"My dad says the same thing," one of the baritones admitted. "He says that homeless people get free rooms and free food without ever having to work for it."

"Exactly," Tressa agreed. "In fact, some of these people give up their homes and live for free in nicer places than they could have if they were working." Tressa looked like she'd won an argument and was proud of it. "Homeless people are just people who want a free ride. The taxpayers like my dad are the ones paying for that ride."

"I've seen the rooms at the mission, Tressa," Mrs. Waverly countered. "They're very small, barely big enough to hold a bed and a chair. What's more, people at the mission are asked to leave during the day because they're supposed to be looking for work. That means that even if they're feeling sick or tired that day, they don't have a choice. They're forced to leave, and can't come back until dinner time."

"You don't need to feel sorry for people like that, Mrs. Waverly. Lots of people who live on the streets prefer that life-style."

"So you're saying homeless people are always homeless by choice?"

"Yeah. I guess you could say that."

"That idea might make you feel more comfortable, Tressa. It's less painful for us to think that the homeless *want* to be that way. It's more difficult to accept the fact that there are no places for them to go, and that we might be responsible for them."

"Why do we have to be responsible for people who choose to live on the street, or waste their lives doing something crazy? Dad says law-abiding citizens are going to have to revolt before things change. We shouldn't have to pick up the bill for other people's mistakes."

The debate that erupted began to turn ugly. Because Tressa was spokesperson for the Hi-Fives, the others of the club sided with her. For the moment it seemed their arguments were winning.

Lexi realized with a pang of guilt how very little she knew about the homeless. She could see Mrs. Waverly's expression turn grim. Lexi supposed that Mrs. Waverly was right. After all, she never told anything but the truth. There probably *were* some homeless people in Cedar River . . . it was just that Lexi couldn't imagine who they might be.

Cedar River was a cozy little cocoon for her life. Lexi didn't like the thought of people without homes disturbing the ideal picture of her city.

Chapter Three

"There she goes again," Jennifer muttered. She and Lexi were standing by their lockers after the last bell, pulling out books for the evening's homework.

Lexi turned her head in time to see Angela Hardy dart through the exit door at the far end of the hallway. It didn't take a detective to notice Angela's quick, furtive steps or the fact that she didn't wear a very warm jacket as she stepped into the chilly wind.

The weather had turned cold. Lexi had begun to get out warm sweaters and a winter jacket from her closet at home. By comparison, Angela's jacket was a lightweight one, which she wore zipped up tightly beneath her chin.

"She sure gets out of here in a hurry," Jennifer groused. "If I hadn't had so many books to carry home, I would have caught up to her this time to find out where she goes."

Lexi could tell by Jennifer's tone that she was in one of her "sleuthing" moods.

"She just flies out of here like she's escaping a plague," Jennifer continued. "She hasn't gotten involved in anything that would keep her after school, like sports or the Emerald Tones, the yearbook or

Review staff. Most kids at least hang around for a few minutes after school. If Angela wants to get to know some of them, she should stay, too."

"You're talking to yourself again, Jennifer," Lexi said. "Maybe she has a job, or something. Maybe she works part time at a fast-food place, or does housecleaning for someone. Maybe she has to get home right away to baby-sit. There are days when I have to leave right away to pick up Ben at the Academy."

Jennifer did not accept Lexi's speculation. "I don't buy any of that. I don't think she has a job." Jennifer slammed her locker shut so hard it shuddered. "I think there's another reason that Angela escapes from the school so quickly every evening. I just don't know what it is . . . yet."

"I wouldn't worry about it, Jennifer. Where Angela goes after she leaves this building isn't any of our business. You're letting your curiosity get the best of you," Lexi said. "Come on. We don't have time to waste. We have to get to the Emerald Tones rehearsal."

"That's another thing I don't like," Jennifer complained aloud. "The entire music department has increased practice time. This concert isn't the end of the world. Why is everyone so worked up about it?"

"We just want it to be good, that's all."

"Well, I'll be glad when it's over. Mrs. Waverly is as nervous as a mouse at a cat convention about this stupid concert. We'll be fine. We always are."

Lexi had to smile. "Maybe even more than fine, now that both Egg and Binky have joined the Emerald Tones."

Jennifer grinned widely. "I never thought those two would make it. I didn't think Egg had a musical bone in his body. What a surprise it was to hear he has such a great voice."

"*Now* he does," Binky said, catching up to her friends. "Egg never tried out before because his voice was always a little . . . touchy."

"What do you mean, touchy?"

"It was changing. You know how it is with guys. One minute their voices are nice and low, the next minute they're high and squeaky. My mom and dad thought Egg's voice was never going to change completely; that he'd be singing soprano one moment and bass the next. My mother says puberty was harder on Egg than on any kid she's ever known."

"Are you sure that's a quote you want repeated outside your family, Binky?" Lexi hid a smile.

"Well, it's true," Binky said matter-of-factly. "If Egg ever completely grows up, it's going to be a miracle."

Neither Lexi nor Jennifer could deny that. When they reached the door to the music room, the chairs were already filling up. Mrs. Waverly stood at the front of the room with a handsome-looking gentlemen—fortyish, and wearing a navy blue suit and red tie. He had a relaxed posture and kept his hands in his pockets while he visited with their instructor.

"Who's that?" Jennifer poked Lexi in the ribs.

"I've never seen him before."

The stranger didn't seem to notice as the kids filed into the room, or how they stared at him curiously with questioning expressions.

"He's nice-looking, isn't he?"

"Handsome, I'd say," Binky peered at the man. "He's got a nice smile. Like a movie star or something."

"He's got even nicer eyes. Did you notice them?"

"It's true, he does have wonderful eyes. Do you see how blue they are?"

"It's not the color that's so special, it's their expression," Lexi murmured. "They look so . . ."

" . . . compassionate?" Jennifer finished for her.

"That's it. He's got the kindest, most compassionate-looking eyes I've ever seen."

"Do you think he's a teacher? Or a music director?" Binky wondered aloud.

"Could be. Or a businessman from uptown. That's how they all dress."

The girls found their seats. After a few moments of scuffling and chair-shifting, everyone was seated. Mrs. Waverly waited until the room was silent.

"Is everybody settled?" she finally asked. "I would like your undivided attention."

Most everyone looked up with anticipation.

"We are privileged to have a special guest with us today," Mrs. Waverly began. "I'd like to introduce to you my friend, Will Adams. I've known him for several months. He has a very interesting story to tell, and I'd like to give him this opportunity to speak to you before we start our rehearsal."

"Thank you." Will Adams smiled at Mrs. Waverly and then at the students. "First of all, I'd like to say that I'm very grateful for this opportunity."

Lexi leaned back in her chair.

"Mrs. Waverly has been telling me about your concert. I'm anxious to hear it. I know what a fine music director you have. The reason this particular concert is special for me is because of the wonderful thing that you're doing by collecting food and money for the needy and the homeless to be shared with them at Thanksgiving. That's going to make this concert stand out from all the rest—your gratitude for the things you have, and your willingness to share from that wealth with people who are less fortunate than yourselves."

"He really is good-looking, isn't he?" Jennifer whispered in Lexi's ear.

All the girls in the Emerald Tones seemed to be admiring Mr. Adams' good looks. He had everyone's attention.

"There needs to be more awareness on the part of the community and the nation about the homeless," Mr. Adams continued.

"Yeah, right."

Lexi winced. That was Tressa Williams' voice.

Mr. Adams fixed his gaze on Tressa. "Do you have a comment, miss?"

Lexi wished that for once Tressa would keep her mouth shut, but that would have been too much to hope for.

"I realize you think it's great that we're collecting all this stuff for the homeless," Tressa blurted, "but I don't think there are that many homeless people in Cedar River. We've had this conversation before," she continued, "and I'm not convinced there should be *any* homeless in this nation. I think the ones who are without homes are that way by choice."

Will Adams' expression grew serious. "Indeed. And what makes you think that?"

Tressa straightened up in her chair and began to recite her litany of beliefs. "There are so many government programs in this country, so many jobs; there's no excuse for anyone to be homeless in this day and age. Homeless people are lazy people. They just don't want to work. That's what my dad says."

Will pulled up a stool and sat down. He rested his hands palms down on his knees as he surveyed the group. "My response might take a few more minutes than Mrs. Waverly had intended for me to speak, but I think it's important that I respond. I'd like to tell you a story—my story. I was homeless myself."

A gasp rippled throughout the room. Tressa's face flushed pink.

"I don't believe that," she blurted. "You look too . . . too nice!"

"And nice-looking people can't be homeless? Is that what you're saying?" Will had a sad look on his face. "There are a lot of misconceptions about the homeless. I'm here to help you straighten them out. The homeless aren't a part of an ugly, uneducated mass of people with whom you can't identify. In fact, many of the homeless are people just like yourselves."

"Not like *me*!" Tressa protested.

"Did you know, for instance, that almost half the homeless adults in America are high-school graduates?"

"You're kidding! If they went to school, how can they be homeless?"

"Each one has a different story. In fact, a lot of the homeless have jobs and go to work every day."

"But if they have jobs, why can't they afford homes?"

"That's not always possible." Will looked more somber than ever. "Many of the homeless have minimum-wage jobs. These jobs pay too little to cover all the expenses a person has—like clothing, food, shelter—especially if they have a family. These homeless can't get ahead. They can't save enough to make a down payment on an apartment or a house. They work to feed and clothe themselves, and live in shelters at night. In fact, some of the homeless are well-trained. They could hold good jobs if those jobs were available. They may have been steelworkers and factory workers who were laid off when the steel mills or factories closed. When the jobs they were trained for disappeared, their incomes also disappeared."

"Are you saying that homeless people have job skills?"

"Not all do. Some don't have any job skills. Some are mothers with young children who don't have a place to leave them during the day. There are also those who have either drug or alcohol addictions or forms of mental illness. My point is that people who are homeless, and their reasons for being homeless, are as individual as each of you are."

"That still doesn't mean that homeless people should mooch off other taxpaying citizens," Tressa countered.

"Yeah, it's just like they're getting a free ride," one of the students in the back row added.

Will shook his head. "Some free ride. It's hardly a ride you would take if it were offered to you."

"But you get free meals."

Will's expression turned to a bitter smile. "Right. Great. Free meals. You stand in line from fifteen minutes to an hour to get a bowl of soup and some bread. You take what they give you. Sometimes they'll put a chunk of cheese on the bread. If you don't like cheese, too bad. You take it because you can't go back and say, 'I'd rather have a bologna sandwich today.' When you've eaten, you can't stop by a pop machine and buy a can of pop or pick up a candy bar, even if you're still hungry or thirsty. You take what they give you and eat it whether you like it or not. At night, when you go back to the shelter, they provide a bed, but it's not like home. Your bathrobe and your slippers aren't waiting for you. If you're lucky, they may have a TV in the lobby you can watch for a while before you go to sleep.

"And, if all of this still sounds pretty good to you, think about doing these things when it's cold outside. Even though you wear everything you own on your back, you're still cold. Maybe you've been wandering the sidewalks all day trying to get warm. Perhaps you stopped for a while in the bus station until someone chased you out. Then you stood in the lobby of a movie theater for a few minutes before they told you to move along.

"Sometimes I went to the library because they didn't chase me away. If you pick up a newspaper or a magazine and go to a far corner to read quietly, they'll leave you alone. If you're lucky, you can stay there until it closes.

"Frankly, I was pretty lucky when I was on the streets. I didn't have to hang around fast-food joints waiting to see if anybody would throw anything away that I could eat. I usually but not always managed to get a roof over my head instead of a cardboard box or a bunch of newspapers. Is that the kind of free ride you want? If it is, you can have it."

When Will was finished, the kids were silent.

Then someone quietly asked, "How did you become homeless in the first place. And how did you become . . . un-homeless?"

"I made several mistakes along the way," Will

admitted. "First of all, I was a hotshot kid and I didn't think I needed to finish high school. I'm from out East, and there was a steel mill in my town. I knew that I could make good money there, so I quit high school and went to work in the mills. That was fine for a while. I bought myself a car, an expensive wardrobe. I was a high flier with my friends.

"Then the mill closed. I thought it would be no big deal to get another job. It took me awhile to realize that not only had I lost *my* job, but so had several hundred men—all trained for the same type of work. None of us could get jobs—anywhere.

"I wasn't very smart about layoffs," Will confessed. "I hadn't saved any money. I was so sure that I'd be able to get another job that I didn't even worry about it. I didn't worry, that is, until my landlord kicked me out of my apartment for not paying my rent.

"I stayed with friends for a while, but soon I became ashamed that I wasn't carrying my own weight, so I moved out. I moved to another city thinking that things would be better there, but they weren't. One thing led to another and pretty soon, I was living on the streets."

"Who helped you?" Minda asked, as involved in Will's story as everyone else.

"There was a church in the city that had a drop-in center. Volunteers from this church cooked meals and fed people three times a day. I started going to the center to eat all my meals—breakfast, lunch, and dinner. I discovered that they would make arrangements with other churches around the city to take homeless people to shelters every night. Churches opened their doors and provided beds for those of us who had nowhere else to go."

Will shook his head, looking grateful even now as he thought back to that time. "I'm so thankful to those people. You have no idea how wonderful it was to stay at a church shelter at night. It was the one place I could sleep in peace and not be afraid of getting assaulted. Every day they made sure that we got showers. Sometimes they even washed our clothes."

A smile creased the corners of Will's mouth. "You hadn't thought about that before, had you? Where the homeless go to wash their clothes and bathe? Usually nowhere. There is no place for them to go. That's why so many of the homeless look so dirty and unkempt. And the more unkempt they are, the more unlikely it is that anyone will hire them. And of course if they aren't hired, they stay homeless."

"Kind of a vicious cycle, isn't it?" Binky blurted.

"A very vicious cycle, young lady." Will smiled brightly. Someone was finally catching on. "But as I said, I am extremely grateful for the people who helped me to break that cycle. They showed me the way out of scrambling for food by day and huddling in a shelter at night. Some helped me to get my high-school diploma, others found funds so that I could start college. I'm proud to say that today I have my college degree."

"Wow! Are you a teacher?" one of the kids asked.

Will shook his head. "No, I'm a social worker. I work with the homeless."

"You mean because you were homeless, you wanted to work with homeless people?"

"It's something I know about, and I see a real need out there. I've been in Cedar River during the past few months helping the mission here to organize an expansion. After all, I've been on both sides of the fence. I know what works and what doesn't. One of my responsibilities is to work with missions and community centers to help them develop the most effective programs for the people they are trying to serve."

"Who are the homeless in Cedar River?" Lexi wondered aloud. "I thought we had a nice community that didn't have people with problems like that."

"You do have a nice community, but no place is without problems. Cedar River has a large migrant-worker population in the summer. Many of those people do not have homes. They come to the mission and community centers for help. And there's usually a large turnover of mothers with young children. Often husbands who are alcoholic or abusive drive their wives and families out of their homes. Those women and children seek safety and refuge at a mission or women's shelter.

"Occasionally, the people are newly homeless. They have lost their home to a fire or their apartment building has been condemned. There are many reasons why people become homeless, but as fellow human beings we can have only one response—that of love and service to those in need."

Will slapped his knees and slid off the stool. "My apologies to your teacher for taking so much of your rehearsal time." He turned to Mrs. Waverly. "Thank you for allowing me to come and visit with your class. My intention was to encourage you with the Thanksgiving project you've started. I didn't mean to burden you with my story, but I do appreciate the receptiveness and honest, forthright questions of this group. And thank you for taking on this project to collect food and money for the needy."

"Thank *you*! I'm sure we've all learned a great deal." Mrs. Waverly shook Will's hand and then walked him to the door. When she turned to the class again, everyone burst out with comments and questions.

"He didn't look like he was ever homeless. He was so well dressed."

"And handsome."

"Being handsome doesn't save you from what life hands you, silly."

"He was homeless when he was our age."

"That's scary. I think I'd better make sure I finish high school."

"Do you think he gave us a true picture about how tough it is to be homeless?"

"Do you think there are really that many homeless people in the United States?"

"This project is a great idea. I'm going to bring twice as much as I'd planned for the boxes for the needy."

"Me, too!"

"We'll do so much there'll hardly be any more poor people in Cedar River!"

The room was abuzz with renewed enthusiasm for the concert. And the enthusiasm showed in their singing.

Chapter Four

It was a lazy Friday evening and the gang had gathered at Lexi's house to bake brownies. Now the counters were wiped off, the baking utensils washed, and everyone sat around the kitchen table eating the finished product, except for Binky, who was busy licking out the frosting bowl.

"Ummm, good frosting, Lexi. I like this new recipe." Binky stuffed the chocolate-laden spatula into her mouth and rolled her eyes with delight. "Yummm."

"Show-off," Jennifer grumped. "Just because it's your turn to lick the frosting bowl, it's especially good tonight, right?"

Binky grinned around the spatula. "You've got it, Golden. We've had some pretty ugly fights at our house over the frosting bowl. I'm going to play this one for all it's worth." Binky looked to her brother Egg for confirmation, but he seemed distracted. He was picking at the crumbs on his plate and staring out the window.

"Hey, tell me about this guy from the mission you heard speak at Emerald Tones practice," Peggy said. "What did the Hi-Fives think of him?"

"They were rude, as usual. They didn't seem convinced by Will that people don't actually *choose* to be homeless."

"Right. Like I'd willingly give up a roof over my head if I had a choice! I don't know what those girls are thinking about. They kept quoting things they'd heard their parents say about people who have 'free will' and those who are 'lazy.' I'm not sure any of them have thought this out. They're just parroting what they've heard at home."

"If that's the kind of thing they're hearing at home, then the homeless aren't going to get much help from people in Cedar River," Binky observed.

"Tressa talked as though homeless people were making an effort to offend her!"

"I don't think Will got through to her. I'm not even sure Tressa actually believed Will was homeless once."

"It's hard to imagine, isn't it? He's so handsome and well dressed. He's educated and intelligent. It hardly seems possible."

"I know, but he said none of us could ever be sure something wouldn't happen to throw us into a situation we never dreamed possible."

"But being homeless?" Binky murmured. "*That* is pretty hard to imagine."

Todd began to feel in his jeans pockets for something.

"What're you looking for, Todd?" Lexi asked.

"This." He produced a piece of paper and proceeded to unfold it and lay it on the table. "After we heard Will speak, I went to the library. I wanted to do a little reading about the homeless."

"Ah, isn't that sweet?" Jennifer poked at the piece of paper. "And you looked things up and wrote them down and made a report for us. What a guy!"

"A report?" Binky groaned. "Who called this meeting anyway?"

"You guys can make fun of me all you want," Todd said. "I learned some pretty interesting things at the library and you're going to hear them whether you want to or not."

"Isn't this Friday? Didn't school dismiss a few hours ago?"

"Just because school's out doesn't mean you can't learn something." Todd ran his finger down the page. "No one really knows how many homeless there are in America, but probably as many as two million."

Jennifer whistled through her teeth. "Wow! That's quite a few. There are entire states that don't have two million people in them, aren't there?"

Todd was intent on the information he had before him. "What's more, every year, more and more of the homeless population includes families."

Binky suddenly looked concerned. "That means there are little kids who are homeless."

"The way Tressa talked, most homeless people are alcoholics or mentally ill," Jennifer pointed out.

"A lot of them are. Probably half. The books I found didn't say for sure, but that still means that there are a lot of people who aren't alcoholic or mentally ill. They're people who've lost their jobs, then their homes because they couldn't pay for them. Many of the homeless are teenagers who've run away, or elderly people who can't make ends meet anymore because they're on fixed incomes. There are also people who are disabled and can't hold jobs."

"That doesn't seem fair at all."

"One book I read estimated that there are at least

one hundred thousand children who don't have homes in the United States."

"Wow, that is hard to believe!" Peggy gasped.

"Yeah, and that doesn't include all the runaways."

"That sounds serious no matter what Tressa or her friends say," Peggy concluded.

"It's serious all right," Binky agreed. "But I doubt there're any homeless people here. Not in Cedar River."

"If there aren't any, what was Will doing in town?"

"Maybe we have one or two homeless people passing through, but I'm sure most of the homeless are . . . somewhere else."

"Binky, you really do have your head in the sand, don't you?" Jennifer said bluntly.

"What do you mean by that?"

"You've been nodding and agreeing with Will Adams all the time, but really you're thinking more like Tressa. You're saying that there are homeless people—somewhere—but not here. Not in your precious Cedar River."

"I've lived here all my life, Jennifer. Don't you think I'd know about something like this?"

Jennifer shook her head. "I used to think that way. I used to think that I knew everything about everybody, but I'm finding out that I don't. If Will Adams says there are homeless people in Cedar River, there probably are."

"Whew," Binky sighed. "Then I don't want to think about it."

"But if Will is right and there are homeless people in Cedar River, then . . . then we have to think about it. We should be doing something about it!" Peggy exclaimed.

"You're right, Peggy," Lexi said. "That's why it's easier to deny that the homeless exist. Then we don't feel guilty and our consciences don't nag us to *do* something about them."

The group carried on an animated discussion for some time before Lexi realized Egg hadn't taken part in any of it. In fact, he'd hardly said a word all evening, and he'd only eaten one brownie.

"Egg? Are you all right?" Lexi asked.

The attention of the group turned to Egg, who until that moment had been gazing dreamily out the window.

"Huh? What did you say? Were you talking to me?" Egg sputtered.

"We've been talking *to* you and *at* you and *around* you for the last fifteen minutes. Where have you been?" Binky snapped her fingers in front of her brother's nose. "And what are you thinking about?"

"Oh, nothing."

"Usually I can believe you when you say that, Egg, but not tonight. You've got a funny expression on your face. You're thinking about something serious, aren't you."

Egg rubbed a hand across his eyes and blinked. "It's nothing. Really."

"Liar. Your nose is growing," Binky taunted.

Egg gave his sister a stern look. "Oh, all right then. If you must know, I was thinking about Angela Hardy."

"Egg's in love!" Binky squealed. "We're having a stimulating conversation about the problem of the homeless, and all you can think about is your crush on a silly girl!"

"I am not in love, Binky."

"You are too."

"Am not."

"Are too. Are too. Are too."

"All right Binky," Todd finally warned. "Don't make your brother mad. You have to go home with him tonight, remember?"

"What exactly were you thinking about Angela?" Jennifer asked, her curiosity getting the best of her.

Egg shrugged. "I don't know. Just how she looks in class, and how quiet she is—and how seldom she smiles." Egg had obviously been observing Angela closely. "I just like her, that's all," Egg admitted, shaking his head innocently. "She's a pretty girl and I think she must be nice."

"Just watch out. That's all I say," Peggy warned.

"Yeah, please don't go crazy like you did over Minda Hannaford," Binky begged.

Egg blushed to the roots of his hair. "I was younger then. I was really stupid. I let a crush on a girl get the best of me."

"You sure did," Jennifer agreed. "You would have done anything to impress Minda—including taking steroids."

Egg looked sheepish, but didn't deny the fact. Everyone knew how close he'd come to getting himself into serious trouble.

"How do you know you like Angela so well? Have you ever spoken to her?" Binky quizzed her brother.

"I've tried. She's hard to catch. I did talk to her at her locker one day—between classes. When she opened her locker door, all her books came spilling out. I stayed to help her pick them up and we talked for a few minutes. She was really nice. She thanked me—and she gave me this—this smile . . ." Egg sighed deeply. "She has the most beautiful eyes I've ever seen. I know she doesn't laugh or smile very often, but that day—she did."

"I've never seen her smile," Jennifer pointed out. "I'm glad to hear she knows how. I thought there was something wrong with her."

"I've thought the same thing," Todd admitted. "Most of the time she looks so miserable you wonder if she's lost her best friend."

"Why don't you guys give her a chance?" Egg blurted. "Why don't you talk to her? Maybe she doesn't feel like she has any friends. Maybe it's your fault she looks so miserable and unhappy. Angela's a great girl, and I'm getting tired of people talking behind her back."

Trouble was brewing. Lexi could see all the warning signs. Egg was going bonkers over the new girl, even though he knew absolutely nothing about her.

"I'm getting tired of this conversation," Todd said impatiently. "Why don't we leave Egg alone? If he wants to fall head over heels in love with some mystery woman, so what? We can always pick up the pieces later. Besides, I don't think Angela Hardy is all that mysterious. She's just a new girl in school who has a hard time making friends. That's all. We're all making too big a deal of this."

"As usual, you're probably right," Lexi said, patting Todd's arm. "We do have a tendency to blow things out of proportion, don't we?"

Todd rolled his eyes. "Just a little."

"I think you're right, Todd. We should change the subject." Peggy slapped the palms of her hands on the kitchen table. "I've got an idea. Let's go moonlight bowling."

"Moonlight bowling? What's that?"

"I saw it in the paper. There's a party at the bowling alley at ten o'clock tonight. Anyone can go and be on a team. They've got food and prizes and music. How does that sound?"

"I'm a terrible bowler," Jennifer said, "but why not? I doubt there'll be any professionals there at 10:00 P.M."

"Sounds like a good idea to me," Lexi said.

Even Egg pulled himself out of his dreams long enough to nod.

"I'll drive," Todd volunteered. "My car's out front. Let's go!"

The bowling alley parking lot was full and the building was buzzing with teenagers inside and out.

"I didn't realize this would be so popular," Peggy said.

"It looks like no one else had anything to do tonight, either," Binky concluded. "Come on. Let's get in line for shoes. Otherwise, they'll run out of my size and I'll have to wear some huge clodhoppers. Lexi, will you find me a ball? Something light. Ten pounds."

While Binky got shoes, Lexi found balls and carried them to their assigned lane. She, Binky, and Egg would be on one team, while Jennifer, Peggy, and a boy named Monte Willis would make up another.

"Hi, Monte," Todd said, thrusting out a hand. "My

name's Todd Winston. "I'm going to be your score-keeper, if that's all right."

"Great. I know you, Todd. I go to Cedar River. I'm just not quite as . . . visible as you are."

Todd laughed. "Yeah, I've discovered you can't hide on crutches."

Monte grinned, and Lexi liked him immediately. He was an easygoing, soft-spoken guy who didn't seem to mind all the banter going on around him.

"I got a strike!" Binky whooped as she watched the pins tumble and fall in every direction. "Look at that, will you? Give me my points, Todd. Boy, am I going to rack them up now."

Unfortunately, the higher Binky's score grew, the lower Egg's remained.

"You're not going to break a hundred if you don't get busy, Egg," Todd warned.

"You're not going to break twenty if you don't get busy," Jennifer quipped.

"You guys talk too much. It's distracting," Egg complained.

"I don't think it's our conversation that's distracting you, Egg. I think it's . . . L-O-V-E!" Jennifer held a hand to her heart. She rolled her eyes and batted her eyelashes. "Love might make the world go 'round, but it makes for a lousy bowler."

Egg took a threatening step toward Jennifer with his ball in hand. "Don't drop that thing on my foot, Egg."

The banter continued throughout the evening, along with some serious conversation about the upcoming concert. Monte didn't seem to pay any attention. When they had wrapped up the final game and were undoing the laces on their bowling shoes, Monte spoke up: "I hope you don't mind my asking, but it was pretty hard not to overhear your conversation this evening."

Egg flushed pink, afraid Monte would refer to the teasing about his love life.

"What was all this talk about the homeless? Do you guys know something about Cedar River that I don't?"

"You've heard of the Emerald Tones?" Lexi began.

"Sure, who hasn't?"

"We're doing a Thanksgiving concert soon. And we're having a food and money drive for the poor and homeless in conjunction with the concert. In school this past week, Will Adams from the local mission came to the Emerald Tones rehearsal to talk about Cedar River's homeless situation."

"That's heavy-duty stuff," Monte said. "I'm impressed. I thought all the Emerald Tones did was sing."

"Oh, we do that too," Lexi said with a laugh. "But this project is something that is catching on, practically by itself."

"That's great." Lexi noticed the respect in Monte's voice. "I saw a special on TV the other night about the homeless in New York City. It was pretty scary. They showed a big warehouse full of cots—rows and rows of them—where the homeless slept." Monte shook his head. "My bedroom's pretty small and junky, but it looks like a palace compared to what they showed on TV."

"*Rows and rows* of cots?" Binky asked, incredulous.

"Yeah. They also showed a soup kitchen. The line

of people waiting for a meal went down the street and around the block. It was really sad. They ran out of food before the line was through and some people were turned away hungry."

"Oh, that's terrible," Binky's eyes grew round. She slumped back against the bench and threw her hands in the air. "It's absolutely hopeless."

"What's hopeless, Binky?" Jennifer asked, used to Binky's dramatics.

"The homeless situation. It's hopeless to help the homeless."

"That's a tongue-twister," Todd joked. "Try saying that ten times fast."

Binky gave him a searing look. "How can you make jokes about something as serious as this?"

"I wasn't making a joke about that . . ."

"You might as well joke," Binky moped. "Feeding and sheltering the homeless is a huge problem; it's impossible for one little person like me to make a difference."

"That's not true, Binky," Monte said. "There's a lot one person can do."

"Oh sure. What, for instance?"

"They said one guy decided to help by bringing food to a homeless person he'd seen huddling in a doorway, and another living in a paper box in an alley. Sometimes all this guy could afford was bread and peanut butter, but he'd make sandwiches and hand them out. Some of his friends heard about what he was doing, and began to get involved. Some cooked. Some delivered the food, and some of them donated money. It all helped. When a church saw what these people were doing, they decided to set up a shelter. Now that church has a soup kitchen, too.

And that same guy still cooks there on his days off, and hands out food to the homeless people who have become his friends."

"What a beautiful story," Peggy murmured. "That means one person really *can* make a difference."

"It's a little like the story of the bread and the fish in the Bible," Lexi commented. "When Jesus had five thousand plus to feed, and all He had was a child's lunch, He used that."

"That's right! It was a miracle. It was enough to feed five thousand, and there was food left over!" Binky enthused.

"Exactly. And God used one man who was willing to share bread and peanut butter, to inspire a whole church to get involved with feeding hundreds."

"Ooohhh, I feel so much better," Binky sighed.

Everyone was feeling pretty good when a loud, excited voice interrupted their thoughts.

"Bowling! Who goes bowling anymore, anyway? Just geeks and nerds and dorks."

Minda and the Hi-Fives came sauntering through the bowling alley, pointing and laughing. They were dressed as if on their way to a party. Lexi had a hunch they'd come just to see if they could stir up a little trouble.

"Well, look who's here. Lexi Leighton and her gang. I guess they fit the bowling description." Gina was being particularly mouthy tonight.

Lexi ignored her.

"Lay off, you guys," Todd commented. "We know you're in here to stir things up."

"Todd's got us all figured out," Tressa said with a smirk.

Todd gave the girls a big grin. "Drop your act and come over and talk to us."

Tressa blinked, looking startled at the invitation, but Minda sauntered over.

"Hi, Egg. How are you?" she said in a provocative tone, squeezing his shoulder lightly with her fingers. Minda probably enjoyed flirting with Egg because he always had a flustered response. But tonight he hardly seemed to notice her.

"Hands off, Minda," Egg said sharply. "You're wrinkling my shirt."

"What?" Minda gasped. "Are you okay, Egg?"

"Why? Because I'm not jumping like a little puppet when you speak? I'm doing great, thank you."

Minda was obviously startled by Egg's mood. He'd played the part of an adoring puppy for so long, Minda couldn't comprehend this new, confident person. Her eyes grew wide and she turned to her friends who looked equally amazed.

Lexi could tell Minda was offended that Egg no longer seemed attracted to her. In fact, she set out immediately to remedy the situation.

"Egg, you're looking awfully handsome tonight. Did you have a good bowling score?"

"No," he admitted, making no effort to impress her.

"You must have had a bad night. I'm sure you normally do really well. Did you get any strikes?"

"No."

"Spares?"

"No."

"It was probably the alley. Warped or something," Minda said, consolingly.

"I'm a lousy bowler, Minda," Egg said bluntly. "I

don't think it has anything to do with the alley."

It was difficult for Todd and Lexi to keep from bursting out with laughter. Poor Minda! She looked so confused. She was pouring on the charm and Egg wasn't responding.

Egg looked confused, too; befuddled by the fact that when he really didn't want Minda around, she was sticking like glue. Finally, to avoid feeling any more awkward, Egg stood to his feet.

"Excuse me, but I have to . . ." He flushed red and stuck a finger in the collar of his shirt, ". . . use the rest room." No one but Lexi seemed to notice that he fled in the opposite direction of the men's room.

"How rude!" Tressa blurted.

Minda waved a hand in the air. "Never mind. He was just having a bad night. I'll talk to him later." Minda led the way, and the other girls followed her across the room.

When they were out of earshot, the gang broke into laughter.

"Did you see the look on Minda's face? Egg had her more confused tonight than she's ever been in her whole life," Binky said with relish. "She obviously doesn't know Egg has fallen out of love with her and into love with Angela Hardy."

"When she gets wind of that, she's going to be mad," Todd said.

"Why? Minda doesn't want my brother."

"She doesn't want anyone else to have him, either," Jennifer pointed out.

"Poor Egg. He's clueless when it comes to girls."

"Oh, I don't know about that," Peggy countered. "I think Egg understands girls pretty well."

"He understands *us,*" Jennifer emphasized. "But

he may not understand the girls he gets crushes on. There *is* a difference."

Lexi was worried about Egg. He may have suddenly and miraculously gotten over Minda, but her instincts told her this new girl would be just as hard to catch. Lexi didn't want Angela Hardy to hurt Egg, but she had no idea what she could do to stop it.

Chapter Five

Through a fog of sleep, Lexi heard the doorbell ring the next morning. It was Saturday, and she groaned and buried her face more deeply into her pillow. Then she heard the muffled sound of the front door opening and little Ben saying a bright "Hello."

"Too early," Lexi muttered, pulling the quilt up over her head. Then Ben rapped at her door.

"Wake up. Lexi's got company."

"Go away," Lexi mumbled. "I'm sleeping."

"No you're not. I hear you."

"Who is it?" Lexi asked wearily.

"It's me, Jennifer."

"Go away. It's too early." Lexi buried her head under her pillow as she heard her bedroom door open.

"Rise and shine, sleepyhead."

"Mmfpt."

"You're wasting the day," Jennifer teased, pulling the quilt from the foot of Lexi's bed.

Lexi screeched in protest as Jennifer started tickling her feet. "No, no! Ach! Eek!" Lexi kicked and flailed.

Jennifer was relentless.

"Let go! No! That tickles!"

"Are you awake yet?"

"Aaah! Yes! Stop! Stop!" Lexi rolled over and Jennifer darted out of the way.

"You'll thank me for this, Lexi. Otherwise, you might have slept the day away."

"Yeah, right. Thanks—for nothing." Lexi stretched like a cat. "What are you doing here so early, anyway?"

"It's after ten o'clock."

"It's Saturday."

"The sun's shining and the birds are singing." Jennifer plopped herself down on Lexi's bed. "Besides, my mom made me get up at seven to do chores. I've been awake for hours."

Lexi rolled over and squinted at Jennifer through narrowed eyes. Her friend's long blond hair was pulled up and to the side in a pony tail. She wore a plain white sweatshirt and acid-washed jeans.

"What's on your mind?" Lexi stifled a yawn. There was no use fighting it. Between Jennifer and Ben, there would be no more sleep today.

"Egg, I guess," Jennifer admitted.

"Egg? You woke up thinking about Egg? That doesn't sound like you, Jennifer."

"Of course not. But considering the circumstances . . ."

"What do you think?"

"Angela Hardy is just too mysterious for my taste, Lexi. There's something really strange about her, and I still can't figure out what it is."

"Give it up, Jennifer. We've made too big a deal over it already."

"But, Lexi, she's so unfriendly. What does she have to hide?"

"Maybe nothing. Why are you so suspicious?"

"Because there are reasons to be. She speaks to no one. She rushes through the halls avoiding any eye contact. And she leaves school every single day as soon as the final bell rings."

"Who would hang around school if they didn't have to? Besides, she comes early enough. Maybe she's tired and just wants to get home."

"But that's strange, too. Why does she come to school so early in the morning?"

Lexi had to admit she'd thought it odd to find Angela in the rest room getting ready for school. She'd never mentioned the incident. The fact would be too much for Jennifer to handle.

Lexi didn't like the look in Jennifer's eyes. "Whatever you're thinking, Jennifer, I already know I don't like it."

"Oh, Lexi, you're such a worrywart."

"I have every reason to be, knowing you," Lexi muttered as she rolled out of bed. She reached for the bathrobe Jennifer had allowed to fall on the floor.

"On Monday, I'm going to follow Angela home from school and see where she lives," Jennifer announced. "I want to know why she's in such a hurry to get there."

"Oh, Jennifer, don't . . ."

"You can't talk me out of this, Lexi. It's a great plan."

"I don't think you should."

"Hey, it's a free country. I can walk anywhere I want. Even on the same path that Miss Angela Mysterious goes. So lighten up, Lexi."

"Why is this so important to you? I don't understand."

"Egg is my friend, Lexi. He's got one of his crazy

crushes on that girl. I don't want him to be hurt."

Lexi's heart twisted a little. She knew that Jennifer, despite her tough talk, truly loved her friends. Egg's best interests were behind Jennifer's actions.

Still, Lexi felt that it was a mistake to sneak around or to follow Angela. If Angela was secretive, it was no doubt because she had something to be secretive about. Perhaps, like Lexi, she had a handicapped brother or sister at home, one that she had not quite accepted. Lexi knew how tough it was to explain a handicapped sibling to people who didn't understand. Or perhaps Angela had other problems. An unhappy homelife or . . .

Lexi didn't want Jennifer trampling over Angela's feelings. It was not easy to discourage Jennifer when she had her mind set on something, however.

"There's something funny about this girl, Lexi," Jennifer said. "I want to know what it is. Once Egg falls in love, he's absolutely blind to any signal that might tell him there's something wrong with a person. You know how he adored Minda. And there are a zillion things to complain about when it comes to *her*!"

"But Egg will get over it," Lexi pointed out. "He always does. You saw how he ignored Minda the other night."

Jennifer grinned. "It was great, wasn't it?" Then she glanced at her watch. "It's time for me to go, Lexi. I didn't realize how late it was. I told my mom I wouldn't be gone long." Jennifer stood up and stretched. "Now, aren't you glad I woke you up?"

Lexi crossed her eyes and stuck out her tongue. "Yeah, right. Deee-lighted!"

"Gotta go. See you later." Lexi heard Jennifer yell

a cheerful good-bye to Ben as she left.

When the front door slammed shut, Lexi yawned and stretched. Now that she was up, she might as well take a shower.

Downstairs, Lexi pulled two slices of bread from the bread drawer and popped them into the toaster, then poured herself a glass of orange juice. She piled on lots of butter, cinnamon, and sugar—her favorite way to fix toast. But Lexi wasn't hungry. She had a knot in the pit of her stomach that simply would not go away.

No matter what she did the rest of the morning, Lexi couldn't help thinking about what Jennifer planned to do. She was going too far this time. Being an amateur detective was one thing, but this was something else. Lexi thought of Angela as a little frightened animal. The last thing she needed was a hunter stalking her.

Lexi cleaned her room, then tried to occupy her mind with her favorite hobby—sewing. She took out a new pattern for a skirt and debated whether to cut it out of black or bright red fabric. She found it very difficult to concentrate on the pattern layout. Finally, she folded the pattern and put it away. It was no time to try to sew while her mind was so preoccupied. She'd make some terrible mistake for sure.

Lexi was beginning to feel like Jennifer's early morning visit had ruined her day. She moved restlessly around the house until she found Ben in the living room with a coloring book and crayons.

Ben looked up from his work. "Hi, Lexi. Whatcha doing? I'm staying in the lines. See?"

"Nice, Ben. I like the blue trees." Lexi ruffled his hair. "You're quite an artist."

"Ben's an artist!" Ben agreed with great satisfaction.

"And a good one."

Ben laid down his crayons and tilted his head up to look at Lexi. "Do you want to color with me?" he asked.

"I don't know, Ben. I'm kind of restless today. I'm not sure I'd be any good at coloring."

"We could play games," Ben suggested. "Or sing. Row, row, row your boat. . . ."

Lexi chuckled. "You must be desperate for a playmate, Ben. Let's see, what could we do that would be fun? I know, let's go out and visit your bunny."

Ben jumped to his feet. "All right!"

Hand in hand, Lexi and her brother went into the backyard to the small brown hutch where Bunny lived. The little rabbit came bouncing to the side of the hutch wiggling his nose in anticipation.

"Have you got something to feed Bunny, Ben?"

Ben nodded. He always carried a few pellets of rabbit food or a carrot in his pocket, much to his mother's dismay on washday.

"Here you go, Bunny." Ben popped some food pellets through the wire. The bunny nibbled at them eagerly.

"Have you fed Bunny already today, Ben?"

"This morning. He was hungry."

"You fed him before you ate your own breakfast?"

"Bunny's special. I don't want him to be hungry."

"You're a good boy, Ben. You take good care of Bunny."

"I know." Ben stuck a finger through the wire netting and stroked the little rabbit's fur. "I love my bunny."

They played with the rabbit a few more minutes before returning to the back step where the two sat silently, enjoying each other's company. Lexi stared at the sky while Ben tied and untied his shoelaces.

"This is silly," Lexi said finally. "Look at the two of us. We're sitting here like a couple of old statues. We should be doing something fun."

"Doing something fun!" Ben echoed.

"What should we do, Ben?"

"Go see Bunny again?" he asked.

"No, let's take a walk."

"Yes! A walk," Ben enthused.

"We'll go to the park. It's a beautiful Saturday for the park."

"You're right, Lexi," Ben agreed happily.

Lexi found her mother to report their plans, and she and Ben left for the park, only a few blocks away. They walked briskly, singing as they went.

"Here we are," Lexi said, arriving at the open area filled with trees, gravel paths, and park benches. "It's not as pretty now as it is in the spring and summer, but it's still a nice place to be, right, Ben?"

"Right."

Suddenly Ben froze in his tracks. "Shhh," he said, lifting a finger to his lips. "Look!"

Lexi followed her brother's gaze and saw two small wild rabbits hunched in the grass.

"Look how still they are," Lexi said softly. "That's because they're afraid of us."

Ben peered curiously at the rabbits. "Where do they live?"

"They live here in the park."

Ben looked around. "But where's their house?"

"They don't have a house, Ben. They live in holes in the ground."

"But my Bunny has a house."

"That's because he's your pet, Ben. These are wild rabbits. They live right here in the park."

"Don't they get cold and hungry?"

"No. They stay warm in their nests. And they know how to find food to eat in the park. Their mother taught them how to find food and live outside. They will be fine."

Ben began to relax a little. "They're not sad because they don't have a house?"

"No. Because they really do have a house, Ben. You just can't see it."

"Oh. I thought everybody had a real home—even bunnies," he said. Then he turned to Lexi with the most trusting expression she'd ever seen on a child's face. "But God wouldn't let anybody be without a home, would He?"

Lexi was relieved when Ben reached down to pick up an unusual rock near the sidewalk to examine. He'd asked her a question she couldn't answer.

God wouldn't let anyone be without a home, would He?

Lexi knew not everyone *did* have a home; that there were lots of human beings in this world who had no place to call their own. She was also growing more convinced that one of the things that Christians were supposed to do was make sure that everyone had somewhere where they felt welcome.

Will Adams' visit to Mrs. Waverly's class was still vivid in her mind. Even when she was playing with her little brother on a Saturday morning, she couldn't get the Emerald Tones' Thanksgiving food collection or Will Adams out of her mind. Thinking of people who have no place to go, no home, no food, and no one to love them left Lexi with a hollow, sad feeling inside.

Suddenly she looked skyward, her eyes narrowing suspiciously. *Are you trying to tell me something, God?*

Lexi knew how God worked with her. More than once He'd put a thought in her mind and left it there to nag at her until she knew what it was that He wanted her to do. Was that happening now? The issue of the homeless was much too big for one person—or was it?

Lexi was still rolling those thoughts over and over in her mind at church the next morning. She spotted Egg and Binky all dressed up and sitting near the front. Todd sat with his family in their usual place on the right. Lexi and her parents usually sat a few rows back on the left side.

It was odd, Lexi mused, how people picked a spot to sit in church and then went back to it Sunday after Sunday. Human beings were creatures of habit. Even in church, they liked to have a "home" pew to come to where everything felt just right.

"Lexi, is something wrong?" Mrs. Leighton asked as they drove home from church. "Are you feeling all right? We were planning to go out for brunch, but if you're not feeling well . . ."

"I feel fine. I'm just . . . thoughtful today. I really want to go out for brunch." Lexi was glad for the diversion. She didn't want to explain to her mother what was worrying her.

Lexi had the awful feeling that if Jennifer followed Angela, she might find out something dreadful about the new girl. Instinctively, Lexi knew that Angela had enough problems without Jennifer causing even more.

Chapter Six

Monday was a dreadful day at school. Lexi was both nervous and restless as she watched Jennifer. She could see that Jennifer was excited—excited about discovering what Angela Hardy's secrets might be.

At noon in the lunchroom Lexi again tried to dissuade her friend. "Jennifer, why don't you give it up? This plan of yours is dumb."

"It's not dumb, and I'm going to do it no matter what you say."

"Leave the poor girl alone. She's just shy."

"Get real, Lexi. There's a mystery about that girl and I'm going to find out what it is. Egg is involved. He's our friend. You know how sensitive he is. We're the ones that will have to pick up the pieces when his heart is broken."

"I doubt his heart will be broken, Jennifer." Even as she said it, Lexi knew it wasn't true. Sometimes she thought Egg's heart was made of glass. It shattered so easily.

When the final bell rang, Lexi saw Jennifer bolt from her seat and move quickly toward the door.

Jennifer had already exchanged the books in her locker and was heading toward the exit when Lexi worked her way through the crowd toward her own locker.

Suddenly Angela appeared from nowhere and bolted through the outer school doors. Just as swiftly, Jennifer followed, and the two of them disappeared outside.

Lexi groaned with dismay and sank weakly against her locker.

"What's wrong? Aren't you feeling well?" Todd came up behind her, putting his left hand against the locker and his right under her chin. The concern on his face was so sweet that Lexi couldn't help giving him a little smile.

"I'm okay, Todd. Really."

"Get your books," he commanded sternly. "I'm taking you home. I think you're getting sick."

"I'm not getting sick. I'm just a little . . . worked up, that's all."

"I can see that. Get your books. You can tell me what's wrong when we get to your house."

When Lexi and Todd got to the parking lot and to Todd's '49 Ford, Lexi crawled inside and sank wearily against the soft, cushiony seat.

At Lexi's they walked together up the sidewalk and into the house. There was a note on the table inside the front door.

> *Lexi, I'm going to pick Ben up at the Academy and take him to the mall. He needs shoes—again. The child is growing like a weed! Back before dinner. Love, Mom.*

"Want something to eat?" Lexi asked.

"Why not? Just call me Ben—growing like a weed."

In the kitchen, Lexi opened the refrigerator door and they both stood with the cool air wafting over them as they stared at the contents.

"Orange juice. Milk. Half a grapefruit. Ham sandwich. Cold pizza."

"Pizza looks good to me," Todd said. "And the milk."

Lexi nodded and took the pizza and milk from the refrigerator. After setting them on the counter, she pulled two plates and two glasses from the cupboard.

"Is there anything else we need?" Lexi asked as she sat down on a stool.

"Just for you to tell me what's wrong," Todd said.

Lexi hardly knew where to begin. Finally, she just blurted out Jennifer's plan. She reminded Todd of the foolish things that Egg did when he was in one of his love-sick states. Then she told him that Jennifer was following Angela home from school to find out where she lived.

"She's following her home from school?" Todd was surprised. "What a crazy idea."

"You know Jennifer." Lexi threw her hands in the air, then buried her face in them. "When she gets an idea, she's determined to follow it through. Jennifer thinks if she knows more about the girl, she'll be able to protect Egg."

Todd sank against the back of his chair. "The whole thing is crazy, but Egg does need someone to look out for him. You know the reputation he has for doing crazy things when he thinks he's in love."

"Exactly."

Todd was quiet for a few moments, his expression thoughtful. "What does Jennifer expect to find by following Angela home? Has she got any idea what she might be getting into?"

"Who knows? Jennifer's got a vivid imagination, that's all I know. She probably has some wild scenario worked up in her mind. As much as I love Jennifer, I wouldn't want to predict what's going on in her mind right now."

"I guess that means we'll just have to wait and see what happens."

After a few minutes, Todd stood up and ran his fingers through his hair. "I guess I'd better go, Lexi. I don't know what to think. And I don't know what good talking about it will do."

"Me either."

"At least life is never boring," he commented.

"Sometimes I think I could stand a little boredom."

Todd laughed lightly. "See you, Lex."

"See you. Thanks, Todd."

After Todd left, Lexi went to the living room and sat down on the couch. She felt alone and confused. Finally she bowed her head. "Father," she murmured, "I don't know what to do to help my friends. Please be with Egg, Angela, and Jennifer and help them to get to know each other without anyone getting hurt. Help Jennifer to be wise and Egg to be sensible . . . and give Angela whatever it is that she needs to feel better about herself. Thank You. Amen."

Lexi was methodically doing her homework when the doorbell rang at eight o'clock in the evening. She stood up and stretched, glad for the diversion.

Before Lexi could reach for the doorknob, the door

flew open and Jennifer burst in. Her blue eyes were huge as saucers and the expression in them was frantic.

"Jennifer!" Lexi exclaimed. "What's going on?"

"Shhh. Be quiet." Jennifer grabbed Lexi by the arm and dragged her toward the stairs. "Let's go up to your room. Quickly."

"We don't have to go upstairs, Jennifer," Lexi said. "There's no one in the living room . . ."

"No. Upstairs, to your bedroom. *Please.*"

Lexi had never seen her friend this agitated. She could feel Jennifer's hand trembling against her arm. *What on earth has happened to make Jennifer behave like this?* Lexi thought.

At the top of the stairs Jennifer shoved Lexi into the bedroom and closed the door behind her.

"Is there a lock on this door?"

"No one will come in without knocking," Lexi assured her.

"Are you positive?"

"Of course. Even Ben knows enough to respect a person's privacy!"

Jennifer sank on the edge of the bed and put her head in her hands.

"Jennifer, are you all right?"

"I'm all right, Lexi," Jennifer muttered. "But I feel terrible. Just terrible!"

"You'd better tell me what happened," Lexi ordered.

"I wish I'd never done it, Lexi. I should never have followed Angela," Jennifer moaned. "Why didn't you stop me?"

"Stop you? I tried, remember?"

"Yes. And you were right." Jennifer flung herself

backward across Lexi's bed. "I'm so stupid I can't believe it. What's wrong with me anyway?"

"Nothing but enough curiosity to kill about two dozen cats. What did you find out?"

"It seemed like I followed Angela forever," Jennifer began. She sat up and brushed her hair out of her eyes. "Egg was right. Angela *didn't* want anyone following her home. She took this convoluted path through a residential district. Then she went through some shops. It was almost impossible to keep up with her. Once I thought I'd lost her, until I realized she'd gone into a shop. From the corner of my eye, I noticed her coming out of the ladies rest room, so I ducked behind some shelves and waited until she left the building."

"Then what?"

"Angela is good at covering her tracks. After forty-five minutes of walking, we ended up down by the railroad tracks."

"Ooohhh." Lexi knew the area down by the tracks was the poorest part of Cedar River. She had seen many houses with the windows and doors boarded up when she and her father had driven through that part of town. There was talk of restoring and renovating the area, but it was still in the planning stages. Most of the businesses there were bars and pawn shops. The city mission was also located there.

"Why did she lead you down there?" Lexi asked, confused.

"Well, she didn't exactly lead me. She didn't know I was following her. Actually, I was getting a little scared, Lexi. That's a scuzzy part of town. There are some really old hotels down there, and bums hang around on the street corners. Some guy asked me if I could spare a quarter."

Lexi gasped. "It could have been dangerous for you, Jennifer."

"I know, but my mind wasn't in gear at the time. I was so determined to follow Angela that I didn't think about anything else."

"Where did she go then?"

"That's the worst part, Lexi. Angela went into one of those dingy old hotels."

"She did? You mean she lives there?"

"I don't know. I thought maybe she was trying to make sure no one was following her, so I waited outside for a long time. But she didn't come out, Lexi. I think she stayed in that hotel." Jennifer shivered. "It was so gross. Before I left, I went into the lobby just to look around."

"Jennifer, you didn't."

"I'd already gone *that* far. Besides, I knew Angela had gone inside."

"What was it like?"

Jennifer made a face. "It smelled old and stale and . . ." Jennifer gave a shudder. "I think people had been using the corners for a bathroom."

"No! How gross!"

"There were old men sitting in high-backed rocking chairs in the lobby, talking and laughing. One old guy was chewing tobacco and spitting into a big spittoon about two feet from his chair. His aim was terrible. The icky brown stuff dribbled down the outside of the spittoon onto the floor. I almost threw up just watching."

"Oh, Jennifer, I can't believe you went in there." Lexi started to feel sick herself.

The silence between them grew uneasy.

"There's more, isn't there?" Lexi finally asked.

Suddenly Jennifer's eyes began to fill with tears and her lips trembled. She reached for the pillow on Lexi's bed and buried her face in it.

"Oh, Lexi. I feel so awful. She lives there. She actually lives there." Jennifer's voice was muffled by the pillow, and Lexi hoped she hadn't heard right.

"What are you saying?"

Tears were streaming down Jennifer's cheeks. "Lexi, I learned something I didn't want to know and now I don't know what to do about it. Angela Hardy lives in the Prince Hotel. I'm sure of it."

"Just because she went into that building doesn't mean she *lives* there, Jennifer," Lexi reasoned.

Jennifer shook her head. "Lexi, I wasn't going to tell you this. I wasn't going to tell anyone, but I don't think I can keep it to myself. You've got to *promise* not to say anything to anyone, unless you talk to me first."

"All right," Lexi agreed.

"I didn't just go into the lobby of the hotel, Lexi. I snooped around."

"Jennifer!"

"I figured if Angela could be there, why couldn't I? Anyway, I waited in the lobby for a while just to see if Angela would come down again. When she didn't, I started walking around. There were only two doors in the lobby. One led to a back-room apartment. I suppose that's where the manager lives. The other door led to a wide, creaky stairway and hall. It looked like it could have been a really nice hotel at one time.

"Upstairs, there was a big open space with some old couches and broken chairs scattered around. There were doors on the left and right sides of the room and two long hallways behind the open space. I peeked in one open door. It was a big communal-type bathroom with showers and toilets. It wasn't very clean, either.

"Halfway down the hall another door was open. There was an old man sitting on the bed. His head was bowed and his hands were folded between his knees. At first I thought he might be praying, but then I realized he was just sitting there, his shoulders stooped. There was nothing in that little room but a straggly plant in a coffee can. The man's shoes were by the bed and his hat on a hook. I think that was all he owned, Lexi."

"Oh, Jennifer," Lexi whispered.

"I didn't want to be caught. By that time I really needed to find Angela. I went downstairs, and several doors were open. The rooms were a little bigger downstairs, and someone had food cooking on a hot-plate. A couple of little kids came out into the hall. I had ducked around a wall to stay out of sight when I saw Angela come out of a room and walk across the hall to another. She'd taken off her jacket and her shoes. After a couple of minutes, she came back into the hall and began to talk to the little kids. Pretty soon, she picked up a ball and tossed it to one of them. I heard the boy yell, 'Hey, Angie, play a game with us.' "

"What did she say?"

"She said, 'Not now, Robbie. I have to start supper before my mom comes home.' "

"Before her mom comes home?"

"That's what she said. That horrible place is her home, Lexi. I know it is. I saw it with my own eyes."

As Jennifer finished her story the enormity of the

situation began to sink in. "Why would she be living there, Jennifer?"

"I have no idea. All I know is that I regret ever getting the hairbrained idea into my head that I should follow Angela home. I thought she had some big secret to hide, but I never dreamed it would be this! I feel like I've intruded into her life. Angela *does* have something to hide, Lexi. I can understand now why she didn't want to be followed. I wouldn't want anyone to know where I lived if it was a place like that." Jennifer began to cry. "No wonder she's so secretive. It would be impossible not to be ashamed of a place like that."

"I'm sure she can't help it, Jennifer."

"I know that. Still, I had no business doing what I did. I'm so sorry. I had no right to discover Angela's secret. I know now that she avoids getting close to any of us because she doesn't want us to know where she lives! Why did I do such a dumb thing?"

Lexi didn't have any answers—only questions.

Lexi tossed and turned all night. Her dreams were disturbing and her sleep restless. She felt exhausted when her alarm rang and it took a great deal of effort to pull herself out of bed. Even an invigorating shower didn't help. Lexi remembered her grandfather saying once that some mornings he felt like he'd been dragged through a knothole in a toothpick. This morning she knew what her grandpa meant.

"Good morning, Lexi," her mother called as Lexi reached the bottom of the stairs. "I've got waffles ready. Would you like some sausage?" When she looked up she was alarmed. "Lexi, what's wrong? You're so pale."

"I didn't sleep very well. . . ."

"Let me feel your forehead. You must be getting sick."

"I'm okay, Mom. Really."

"Hmmm, no fever. Do you have a headache?"

"No, Mom. I just didn't sleep well last night."

"Did you sleep at all?"

That was closer to the truth than Lexi cared to admit. "I just had some bad dreams. I'm okay. The fresh air will help."

Lexi grabbed a waffle and dunked a corner in the syrup on Ben's plate. "If I leave right now, I can walk. That will wake me up for sure."

"Please call if you feel worse. I'm going to be here all day, and I'll be happy to pick you up."

"Thanks, Mom. Bye." Lexi escaped through the door feeling worried, exhausted, and near tears, but as she got closer to the school, her step quickened. If she got in early enough, perhaps she'd have the opportunity to talk to Mrs. Waverly. Right now, Lexi desperately needed some answers.

Mrs. Waverly was in her office next to the music room, grade books spread out on her desk. Lexi knocked timidly on the slightly open door. "Mrs. Waverly?"

"Yes. Who is it?"

"Lexi. May I come in?"

"Certainly." Mrs. Waverly picked up music sheets from the only other chair. "Sit down, dear. Are you feeling all right? You look pale."

"I know. My mother told me that, too. I didn't sleep very well last night." Lexi was grateful that

Mrs. Waverly didn't ask why. She seemed to have a sixth sense where teenagers were concerned.

"Mrs. Waverly, I have a rather strange question I'd like to ask you."

Mrs. Waverly's eyebrows rose. "Go ahead."

"Have you ever heard of the Prince Hotel?"

"The Prince Hotel? Why, yes. Why do you ask?"

"I was wondering if you could tell me anything about it."

"The Prince Hotel is what Mr. Adams calls a welfare hotel.

"Who lives there?" Lexi asked, hoping Mrs. Waverly wouldn't question her further.

"People waiting for low-income housing to become available. There are usually more people needing such housing than there are homes to go around. One of the projects Will Adams is involved with is finding resources to build more low-income housing. Places like the Prince Hotel are simply not adequate. First of all, they're very old buildings with very small rooms, and secondly, there are no cooking facilities. Unfortunately, there isn't a lot of money available for projects like Will's."

Mrs. Waverly was obviously curious but didn't pry. Instead, she put her arm around Lexi and gave her a hug. "You know, Lexi, if you have questions, you can talk to Will Adams anytime. He's very compassionate and understanding. He's been on both sides of the problem. If there's something about the homeless that disturbs you, go to him. He'll be glad to help you."

"Thanks, Mrs. Waverly. Maybe I will."

"Let me write down the address. Will has a small office in the mission." Mrs. Waverly printed the address carefully and handed it to Lexi.

Lexi clutched the paper tightly and hurried out of the room.

"Lexi, hi," Jennifer whispered.

"Hi, yourself."

They exchanged knowing glances full of emotion.

"Hey, what are you two looking so secretive about?" Egg asked as he walked up to them in the lunchroom.

"Have you two got some news you're not sharing?" Binky followed her brother.

As they sat down at a table in the lunchroom, Angela Hardy walked through the far door carrying her tray. To the amazement of everyone at the table but Lexi, Jennifer's eyes filled with tears. She pushed her tray away.

"I'm not very hungry," she stammered. "Gotta go." She jumped up and hurried out of the lunchroom.

"What's wrong with her?"

"What was that all about?"

Lexi knew exactly what was wrong and stood up. "I think I'd better go and talk to her. Someone take our trays up?" Not waiting for an answer, she hurried off.

Chapter Seven

Neither Lexi nor Jennifer felt much better after school the next day when they met at the lockers.

"How are you doing, Lexi?" Todd brushed a stray lock of hair from Lexi's eyes.

"Okay."

"What's going on with you and Jennifer?"

"I'd love to talk to you about it, but I can't . . . not yet. All right?"

"I'm here for you when you need me, Lexi. You know that." Todd skimmed a kiss across the top of her hair. "Gotta go or I'll be late for class. Talk to you later?"

"Yeah."

"What a day," Jennifer muttered.

"I know," Lexi said. "It's been terrible for me, too."

"Mr. Raddis asked me if I was feeling all right this morning." Jennifer made a face. "Do I look that bad?"

"You look fine. It's the expression in your eyes, I think."

"I feel so helpless about Angela," Jennifer moaned. "I hate having this secret, but I suppose we shouldn't tell anyone."

"It would be an invasion of her privacy," Lexi agreed.

"But shouldn't we say something to *someone*?"

"I don't know. It even hurts to look at her now. I finally understand why she wears old jeans and baggy T-shirts. It's probably all she has. I wish we could help her."

"She acts like a prickly porcupine," Jennifer commented. "She won't let us get near her."

Jennifer and Lexi walked down the hall feeling helpless and sad.

At the doorway of the chorus room, Mrs. Waverly was greeting people and hurrying them to their spots.

"Come in, come in. Sit down. Take your seats. I have exciting news."

When the last of the choir members had shuffled to their seats, Mrs. Waverly took her place in front of the group. "I've had a call from Will Adams, our friend at the mission." Mrs. Waverly smiled broadly. "Will has invited a group from our school to visit the mission. He's so excited about our concert and the collection of food and money which we are sponsoring that he wants some of you to visit the mission and learn what its goals are. He wants a volunteer group—those of you who are interested in learning more about poverty and homelessness in America.

"This will not be a fun excursion, but rather an opportunity for learning. You should all consider it. "Do I have any volunteers?"

Without hesitation, Lexi, Todd, Jennifer, and the rest of their friends raised their hands.

Across the aisle Lexi saw Minda poke Tressa and whisper, "Tressa, you can see for yourself that there really are some poor people in Cedar River."

Lexi held her breath. She didn't want Tressa Williams to go on this trip. Tressa was too outspoken and negative. Lexi was disappointed to see that not only Tressa, but Minda, Gina, and the other Hi-Fives decided to go on the field trip as well.

"Meet tomorrow by the music office after school. I have arranged for transportation to and from the mission," Mrs. Waverly said. "We should be gone about an hour and a half. Please let your parents know where you'll be. We'd better get started on our music. . . ."

After class, as Lexi headed to her locker, she caught sight of Angela in the hallway. A dart of pain shot through her. *Oh, please,* she murmured to herself. *Don't let Angela's secret get out.*

The next day, the hours until lunchtime seemed to stretch on forever. Lexi wasn't hungry. There was a knot in the pit of her stomach, and she couldn't concentrate in class.

As she walked down the hall after the final morning bell, Lexi heard a voice and footsteps behind her. "Lexi, wait up. Wait for me."

Egg was jogging toward her, his eyes bright.

"What happened to you? Straight A's? You found a hundred-dollar bill in the hallway? I haven't seen you look so happy in a long time."

"The greatest thing just happened, Lexi." Egg was beaming. "I finally caught her!"

"Caught her?" Who?"

"Angela Hardy."

The knot in Lexi's stomach lurched. "Oh?"

"This morning after second-hour class. We entered the hall at the same time and I accidently bumped into her. I apologized, and she turned to me and smiled. She has a beautiful smile."

"So that's how you caught her?"

"Oh, no, it was better than that. She dropped one of her books and I picked it up for her. My mind was whirling a hundred miles an hour because I knew I wouldn't have much time with her. So I hung on to her book. I looked her straight in the eye and said, 'Angela, you look like a really nice girl. I'd like to get to know you better. Would you go out with me?' "

"Egg, you didn't!"

"I did. Isn't it great, Lexi?" He grinned widely. "And you know what else? She said yes!"

Lexi was shocked. "Where are you going on your date?" she asked cautiously.

"Bowling. She loves to bowl. Isn't that wonderful?"

If Egg had been a puppy dog with a new toy he couldn't have been more excited.

"You're going to pick her up and take her to the bowling alley?"

A frown crossed Egg's face. "No, not exactly. Angela didn't want me to pick her up. She said she'd meet me at the bowling alley."

"Oh?"

"Yeah, I'm not sure I like that. I'd like to meet her parents, but Angela said her mom isn't home very often and it would be so much easier for her if we met there." Egg shrugged. "I said it was fine. I really don't care where we meet, Lexi. I've got a date with Angela!"

As he walked away, Lexi was sure Egg was floating six inches off the floor. She was also sure the knot in the pit of her stomach was not apt to go away any time soon.

Her friends were already at the lunch table when Lexi arrived. Egg was holding court. There was a blissfully satisfied smile on his face as he told everyone about the grand moment when he'd asked Angela out on their date.

"Egg, old man, it looks like you're falling head-over-heels in love," Matt concluded as he forked up the last of his macaroni and cheese. "Don't get yourself in too deep like you did with Minda. You were downright sappy about her."

"Angela's different, Matt. I know she is. She's the kind of girl who could care about me. You can just see it in her eyes." Egg sighed and looked off into space. "She has the most beautiful eyes. . . ."

"I don't like this, Egg," Binky said. "You don't know anything about her."

"Quit sounding like Mom and Dad. You're my sister, not my parents."

"Sometimes I think you need more than our parents to keep you in line, Egg," Binky countered. "Don't you see it? Because you're crazy about her, you only see the good in Angela. There are probably some bad things about her that you don't see."

Jennifer and Lexi exchanged worried glances.

"She's not friendly with the rest of us, you know. We've tried to talk to her and she always avoids us. She's . . ." Binky sought the right word. ". . . she's mysterious! That's what she is."

"Mysterious, Binky? Get real."

"It's true, Egg! She leaves school in the afternoon like she's been shot from a cannon. And she never gets involved in anything outside of classes."

"You're being too critical, Binky," Egg said. "We talked. I understand her."

"You do?" Lexi looked surprised. "What do you understand?"

"Angela's had a hard time, Lexi. I shouldn't tell you this, but you guys are being so hard on her I feel like I have to defend her."

"Hard time? How?"

"Angela told me that her mom lost her job not long ago. She's been looking for work, and Angela's worried about her."

Lexi and Jennifer looked at each other again. Was that all that Angela had told Egg, or had she told him the rest of the story? Lexi doubted Egg could have sat there smiling if he'd known that Angela and her mother lived in a welfare hotel in the poorest part of Cedar River.

All those who had volunteered to visit the mission met after school at the music office. Most of the Emerald Tones were there, as well as several people from Lexi's history class.

Mrs. Waverly was busy directing everyone to the bus outside. "Please file out quickly and take a seat. We don't have any time to waste."

The group rushed outside, and after some pushing and shoving, everyone managed to get on board.

Minda and the Hi-Fives took control of the backseats. Lexi, Todd, Egg, Binky, and Jennifer were close to the front. The noisy banter and laughter subsided as they neared the mission.

"My family never comes down here," Tim Anders

remarked. "This place needs a neighborhood cleanup project."

"Look at all the junk in the streets."

"The buildings are so dingy. They need some paint and some shrubbery or something to brighten them up."

The area had a depressing effect on the whole group. They were all silent when the bus pulled up to the mission doors.

It was a clean building with large windows, and a welcome sign posted out front. The hours were listed beneath it. Another sign read *Jesus Loves You*.

The subdued group filed through the doors and were greeted by Will Adams. He was dressed in jeans, a black turtleneck, and a plaid wool shirt. He looked genuinely happy to see everyone, and shook their hands as they entered the room.

"Welcome! Welcome, everyone. I'm glad you all came."

Lexi knew the man cared deeply about the homeless and was anxious to interest others in the cause.

"I'd like to start with a tour of the building and tell you a little bit about what we do here."

They entered the dining room, where long tables were set with mismatched chairs. The room was sunny, with bright yellow curtains at the windows. A small radio played music in the corner. Everything was spotless.

"This is where we serve our meals," Will explained. "The kitchen is just behind those doors. We'll look at that in a few minutes. All our labor here is done by volunteers. Some of the people who stay here also help with the cooking and the cleaning."

"A lot of people actually live here?" Tim asked.

"The number varies," Will said. "Some come only for meals, others stay longer. Especially in the winter, of course. Life is hard on the streets anytime, but much more difficult once the weather turns cold."

"People live *outside*, even in the winter?"

Will chuckled. "I did. I had a cardboard box, which provided a bit of protection."

A gasp rippled through the room.

"Many of the homeless sleep in cardboard packing boxes. They feel very lucky if they can find a refrigerator or washing machine box, because they're large enough to stretch out in."

Despite the disbelieving stares from some in the group, Will continued. "Best of all, if you have a nice large cardboard box and a warm air grate to put it over, you can sleep almost comfortably."

"You've actually spent winter nights like that?"

"Yes."

"What did you eat?"

"The same as every other homeless person—whatever I could find. If you don't have access to a soup kitchen or they run out of meals before they get to the end of the line, you scavenge through the garbage or beg for money."

"You did that too?"

Will looked serious. "I did it all, son. Once I saw a man cleaning out the back of his car. He threw two half-eaten sandwiches in plastic bags into the garbage. I hardly waited for him to drive off before I took them out of the garbage can. I was so hungry, I didn't care what anyone thought if they saw me."

"Did you get sick?"

Will chuckled. "At that time in my life, I had so

much foreign bacteria in my stomach I wouldn't know what made me sick and what didn't. All I knew was that I had to eat, and if there was food around I ate it."

"How long did you live like that?"

"A long time. It was only when I got into a mission similar to this one that I started to believe that I could get back on my feet. I still remember it. The organization was housed in the basement of a large church in New York City. It was a warm, friendly place that offered a bed and a meal every evening, no questions asked. Their motivation was Matthew 25:35–40: 'I was hungry and you gave me food. I was thirsty, and you gave me something to drink. I was alone and away from home and you invited me into your house. I was without clothes and you gave me something to wear. I was sick and you cared for me. I was in prison and you visited me . . . I tell you the truth. Anything you did for any of my people here, you also did for me.'

"They believed they were serving God by serving the homeless. I went there every night for a warm meal, a shower, and a place to sleep. Once I became a regular, they assigned me a locker so I could store what few things I owned without the fear of being robbed. After breakfast I'd go out into the streets again."

"Was the place just for men?"

"They had a shelter for women also."

"And children?"

"Yes. The women's shelter provided for them and their children. They were even allowed to use the shelter's address as their own, so that they could receive government assistance. Without an address, you are not eligible for food stamps and welfare."

"Can it really be that hard with the government handing out welfare checks?" Tressa asked, as insensitive as ever.

"If everything you own is taken away from you and you are left to fend for yourself on the streets, everyday activities become difficult. Without cash, you can't rent an apartment. And if you're hungry and without clean clothes you can't impress a prospective employer, either."

Tressa couldn't argue with that.

"I could tell you dozens of stories of families who were forced to leave their homes because the wage earner lost his or her job. Without a job they couldn't pay their rent. Some families move in with relatives. But that sort of arrangement doesn't always last for long, and they have to look for something else.

"That's where the missions and shelters come in." Will smiled at the somber faces. "I don't mean to depress you, but you should know the plight of the homeless and what missions and shelters do for them.

"The Thanksgiving concert and food drive is an important contribution by you students and the rest of the community.

"I've discovered another advocate of the homeless here in Cedar River. Do any of you know Pastor Lake?"

Lexi's hand went up, along with several of her friends.

"Pastor Lake has agreed to set up a food pantry at his church as part of the Homeless Awareness Program that I'm starting. I realize you'll be taking canned goods to the concert, but if you wish to continue to provide food during the year, you can take it to the church food pantry."

Those from Pastor Lake's church seemed interested in the possibility of providing food items throughout the year.

"Unless you have more questions, I'll show you the kitchen next, and then the lounge and rooms where people spend the night."

Lexi glanced over to Egg, who looked particularly distressed. It was all he could do to hold back the tears, and he waved to Lexi as he moved toward her. "Lexi, do you know where the rest rooms are?" he whispered.

"I saw signs when we came in. I'll show you."

While the others looked at the mission kitchen, Lexi and Egg made their way to the rest rooms. Just as they turned down a hallway, they were stunned to come face-to-face with Angela Hardy.

"Angela," Egg gasped. "What are you doing here? You weren't on the bus, were you?"

The look of dismay and horror on Angela's face left Lexi speechless.

"No, I—uh," Angela stammered.

Just then, a voice came from the stairs. "Angela? Are you there? I need you to run a couple of errands for me before supper. You'll have to go right now, so we're not late for the meal."

Angela's face blanched white and her voice quivered. "Coming, Mom."

Egg stared at Angela. "You . . . you live here?"

"No . . . my mom works here. I've gotta go."

Egg touched her arm. "Is this why you didn't want me to pick you up at your house?"

Tears welled up in Angela's eyes, but she didn't speak.

"Why didn't you tell me?" Egg pleaded. "I would have understood."

"Would you still have wanted to go out with me if you knew I lived in a welfare hotel?" Angela blurted. She whirled and ran up the stairs. "You can forget about our date," she called from the top of the stairway.

Egg seemed chiseled in stone as he stared blankly at the empty stairs. Usually when he was upset, he was agitated and noisy. Now he was quiet, cold, and hurt.

By the time they returned to the dining room, Mrs. Waverly was calling for everyone to board the bus. Lexi took Egg's hand and walked him toward the door. Without a word, they mounted the steps and took a seat together.

Todd looked at Lexi, puzzled that she would sit with Egg. But he also noticed Egg's expression, and knew that something was dreadfully wrong.

Everyone else was too wrapped up in their own emotions and impressions of what they had just seen and heard to notice Egg. Even Tressa was subdued.

When they arrived back at Cedar River High School, it was a quiet group that left the bus. Egg had absolutely nothing to say.

"Come on, you guys!" Peggy stood in the doorway of her bedroom holding a pizza and glaring at her friends. "It's Friday night and we're having a slumber party. You're acting more like it's quiz time on a Monday morning. Why is everyone so glum?"

Binky sat in front of the mirror methodically putting rubber bands in her hair and pulling them out again. "I hate my hair. It's ugly."

"Well, you're lucky it's only your hair you hate. I hate myself!" Jennifer flung herself across the bed, and Lexi knew what was coming next.

All week Jennifer had been feeling more and more distressed about the fact that she had followed Angela after school. Lexi understood. She had been keeping to herself the fact that Egg had discovered Angela was homeless and living near the mission. These were secrets neither of them could keep much longer.

"What do you mean, you *hate* yourself?" Peggy asked. "I've had lots of counseling. Maybe I can help you."

"I did something stupid," Jennifer admitted. "Now I can't forgive myself."

"What did you do? Rob a bank? Steal a car?"

"Worse."

That got Binky and Peggy's attention. "What do you mean?"

Suddenly Jennifer spilled the whole story.

Peggy and Binky registered their shock. But it all seemed possible now that they'd visited the mission and heard Will Adams tell them more about the homeless.

"Poor kid!" Peggy shook her head. "No wonder she's so quiet in school." Then a horrified expression crossed her face. "You haven't told anyone else, have you, Jennifer?"

Jennifer shook her head. "No. And it's news that shouldn't be spread, especially to the Hi-Fives. The last thing Angela needs is to be teased and taunted about being homeless."

"Did *you* know about this, Lexi?" Binky asked.

Lexi nodded and told them about her and Egg meeting Angela at the mission.

"That's it!" Binky blurted. "That's why Egg's been acting so strange all week."

"I guess we're pretty ungrateful for all the things we have," Peggy remarked.

"Whew! Boy, do I feel selfish," Binky admitted.

Lexi felt a little guilty for not having let Binky in on their secret, since it involved her brother.

"Egg's been researching stuff in the library about the homeless. Now I know why he's so angry."

"Angry?" Peggy echoed. "That doesn't sound like Egg."

"Yes, angry. He's taking it all so personally—because of Angela and how he feels about her." Binky looked at her friends with wide eyes. "I'm scared. Really scared."

"What are you scared of, Binky?"

"Egg is going to do something weird, I just know it. You know my brother. He's been known to go too far in the past. I can't even imagine what he might try now."

Chapter Eight

Clink.

Clink, clink, clink.

The sharp tapping sound intruded Lexi's restless sleep.

Clink . . . clink.

Lexi buried her face in her pillow. *Must be raining outside—but that clinking sound on the window doesn't sound like rain.* Lexi lifted her head. *Hail?*

Clink, clink, clink.

Lexi yawned and stretched. As she did, her feet brushed against Binky's shoulder. Lexi peered over the mound of blankets. Binky was sprawled across the foot of the bed, her arms hanging over one side, her toes over the other. She was snoring like a kitten.

Lexi sat up and rubbed her eyes. It took her a second to remember that they'd spent the night at Peggy's. It had been late when they finally all crashed and slept wherever they landed. Binky had made it to the foot of the bed; Jennifer was rolled up in a thick comforter on the floor; Peggy was curled into a ball on the other side of the double bed Lexi was in.

Clink. Clink.

There it was again. Lexi, fully awake now, was puzzled.

"Binky, wake up." She prodded at her with her toe. "Binky, do you hear that?"

"No. Stop poking me."

Lexi leaned over and shook Peggy's shoulder. "Peggy, there's a strange noise at the window."

"You're the strange noise. Be quiet and go back to sleep."

"I'm serious. Listen."

Clink. Clink. Clink.

Peggy rubbed her eyes. "It's raining outside," she mumbled.

"No, it's not."

"Can you people be quiet up there?" Jennifer growled from the floor. "You woke me up."

"Jennifer, do you hear that strange sound? What do you think it is?"

Clink.

"I don't know."

"It's something at the window," Binky yelped. "Now will you please be quiet and let me sleep?"

"We're on the second floor. What's going on?"

Suddenly, all four girls were wide awake and wading through the tangle of blankets to the window.

"There's nothing out there," Binky stated flatly.

Clink.

"Hey! Somebody's throwing stones at the window!" Peggy shouted. "Did you see that?" She turned the latch and threw open the window. "Whoever is throwing stones—stop—now!"

Binky gasped. "It's Egg! Egg McNaughton, you are the world's strangest brother. What in the world are you doing here and why are you throwing stones at Peggy's window?"

"What's happened to him?" Lexi exclaimed. "He looks awful!"

Egg stood in the flower bed beneath Peggy's window, dressed in old jeans and a baggy, torn coat. His hair stood straight up in spiky clumps. One cheek was smudged with dirt, and his eyes looked glassy and bloodshot.

"He looks like he's going to faint," Peggy remarked.

"Let's go downstairs and bring him inside."

The four girls grabbed robes and raced for the stairs.

"Shhh! Don't wake my parents. It's too early," Peggy warned.

"What do you think he's doing outside at this time of morning looking like he spent the night in a garbage can?" Jennifer whispered.

"Who knows?" Binky muttered. "He's my brother."

The rest of the Madison household was dark and quiet. Peggy switched on a light in the kitchen, then opened the door. "Egg, get in here," she whispered hoarsely.

With slow, faltering steps, Egg moved toward the door.

"You look like a zombie!" Binky croaked.

Lexi noticed dark shadows beneath his eyes and across his cheekbones. Strangest of all was the expression on Egg's face. It registered exhaustion and misery. Lexi thought he was going to cry.

"I think you'd better sit down before you fall down," Jennifer ordered, pulling out a kitchen chair. Egg sank onto it without a struggle.

"Do you want something to drink? orange juice?"

Peggy pulled a carton from the refrigerator. She looked at her friends. "I think we all need to eat something."

Peggy poured juice and put a package of muffins on the table, while Lexi, Jennifer, and Binky surrounded Egg, demanding to know what happened.

Egg was silent, oblivious to the girls' prodding and questions. Then he put his head in his hands and massaged his scalp with his fingers. When he looked up, his eyes were damp.

Lexi put a hand on his arm. "Egg, you have to tell us what happened. You're scaring us. Look at Binky. She's practically shaking."

Egg reached for the orange juice and swallowed it in one gulp. "Let me eat first. I'm going to need some strength for this."

The girls pulled their chairs around the table and joined him. Egg devoured one muffin after another like he hadn't eaten in days. When he finished those, he reached for the toast Peggy was making.

Finally Egg raised a hand. "That's enough for a while. I'm full. Thanks."

"I've seen football players eat less than that for breakfast," Jennifer commented.

"I was hungry," Egg stated simply. He looked sad and pitiful.

"The time has come, Egg. Spill it!" Binky demanded.

"I'm impulsive, I know," he admitted. "I realize that sometimes I act before I think. It's really stupid of me, but I can't help it. It's just how I am."

"We know how you are, Egg," Binky said impatiently. "What does this have to do with last night?"

"Last night I couldn't quit thinking about Angela," he began. "I thought of her living in a welfare hotel. I imagined her coming to school and trying to be elusive so that no one would find out where she lived or what her situation was." His eyes glazed. "I felt so sorry for her and so helpless! I didn't know what to do for her.

"I realized that I didn't understand the homeless. Until recently, I didn't even know there were any around Cedar River. Now, all of a sudden, I'm seeing signs of it everywhere. Did it happen that quickly or have I been blind until now?"

"Maybe a little of each," Jennifer suggested.

"I couldn't forget Angela and the things I'd learned about her. I tried to understand how she must feel so I could be sympathetic toward her, but I couldn't imagine how it would feel to be homeless.

"I tried. I pretended I was hungry, but then I remembered I'd just eaten three pieces of pizza. When I tried to pretend I was homeless and there was no place for me to go, it didn't work, because I was sitting in my own bedroom with blankets and pillows and clothes and music all around me. I just couldn't do it."

"It's not your fault, Egg. You've never had to live that way." Lexi tried to sound reassuring.

"Anyway, my crazy idea started when the folks called and said they were staying overnight with my grandfather. I knew Binky would be here with you guys, so that left me all alone.

"After I finished my homework, I tried to read, but I couldn't concentrate. Everyone I called was out or busy. Todd was with his brother Mike, and Matt wasn't home. I seemed doomed to think about everything Will Adams had said, and about Angela not having a real home. That's when I decided to find out what it was like to be homeless."

"Egg McNaughton! You idiot!" Binky gasped.

"I found some old clothes in the basement. I put on two pairs of long underwear so I'd be warm, and—" Egg looked sheepish. "I ate three bowls of cereal and two sandwiches so I wouldn't get hungry. I guess that's cheating. When you're homeless, you don't have that opportunity. Then I went down to the mission area and walked around, imagining what it would be like if I didn't have my home to go to or my family and friends. I tried to imagine what it would be like to be hungry. That was a little tough until later in the night."

"And you just wandered around down there?" Jennifer asked.

Egg nodded. "It's really different in that part of town after dark. Everything comes to life. There are bums on the street drinking from bottles they've pulled out of paper bags. Music in the bars gets real loud, and the people inside are dancing, playing cards, carrying on all night."

"Egg," Lexi chided, "you could have gotten hurt down there."

"Lexi's right, Egg," Jennifer said sternly. "You could have been clunked on the head. Your wallet might have been stolen."

"I didn't have a wallet. I left all my money at home. I was trying to see what it was like to be homeless, remember?"

"So you were downtown, in ragged clothes, with no money and no identification?" Binky scolded.

Egg looked sheepish again. "When you put it like that, it sounds pretty stupid."

"That's because it *is* pretty stupid, Egg."

"Maybe so, but I was no different than a lot of other people down there. There were others who must not have had identification, money, or a place to go." Egg's expression changed. "It was scary. Really scary. For the first time I saw how tough life could be for the homeless. It was a stupid, dangerous thing to do—I realize that now. But you know me, I always act first and think later."

"Or don't think at all," Binky muttered.

"What else happened?" Peggy demanded. "Now that you've had the experience, let's not waste it."

Egg shot her an appreciative glance. He didn't need or want any more scolding. He was feeling chastised and humiliated enough already.

"At first, I walked up and down the streets, just looking around and watching people. Just before midnight, I realized that these places might be closing soon, and I wouldn't have anywhere to go." He shuddered. "It was getting colder too. I thought these long johns would keep me warm, but it didn't work out that way." He looked at his sister. "And you know how I like a midnight snack? All of a sudden, my stomach started growling."

Egg looked crestfallen. "I'd be a lousy homeless person, wouldn't I? Four hours on the street and I was already cold and hungry. I realized almost too late that I'd have to find somewhere to sleep if I was actually going to go through with this. I also realized that I should have made plans during the day. I didn't dare go to the mission. Will might have recognized me. But there were some guys going to sleep in an alley. They had refrigerator boxes, like Will mentioned."

A strange expression came over Egg's face. "One guy was sleeping in a big-screen TV box. That seemed really crazy to me. Here was a guy who didn't even have a roof over his head, while somewhere, somebody was watching a late news report about the homeless on their big-screen TV, while this guy was sleeping in the box it came in!" Egg had a sad, faraway look on his face. "It's hard to imagine that people in the same country, at the same moment, can be having such totally different experiences."

Egg had changed overnight. This brief experience had opened his eyes to things he'd never realized before.

"Finally some guy took pity on me and told me where he'd gotten his cardboard box. He said there were some smaller ones left if I wanted one. There were only three boxes in the dumpster, but I pulled them apart and managed to make a tent out of them." Egg shivered. "I see now why they put those boxes over heat grates in the street. I don't think there's anything colder to sleep on in the whole world than concrete—or harder, either."

"Weren't you frightened?" Peggy asked.

"I was terrified. By 2:00 A.M., I'd finally gotten settled inside my cardboard tent." His lip twisted in a humorless smile. "It's weird, but I understand ostriches now—why they bury their heads in the sand. When I pulled the flap of the box over my head and shoulders, I felt safer. It was like because I couldn't see the danger, it wasn't out there."

"Oh, Egg!" Binky was almost crying.

"But I was reminded of where I was when a drunk stumbled over me during the night. My boxes collapsed and the guy was all over me. I screamed and he fell off. As soon as I smelled his breath, I realized I had nothing to fear. The poor guy was having trouble standing up. He'd tripped on my big feet sticking out the end of my tent."

"You could have been hurt! You could have been killed!" Binky wailed.

"What did you do then?" Peggy asked.

"I got up and arranged the boxes over the poor guy. He'd passed out, and I thought he should be kept warm."

"So you gave up your boxes for him?" Jennifer asked, looking truly impressed.

"I knew I couldn't sleep anymore, anyway. Besides, he needed it worse than I did. After all, I *did* have a home I could go to. I got up and started walking. I had plenty to think about. I never dreamed being without a home could be so terrible. In my wildest imagination, I had no idea . . ."

Tears spilled onto Egg's cheeks. "I was so frightened and felt so alone—and I had a *home*! If the street had been my only home, I think it might have been easier for me to just lie down and die."

"Oh, Egg." Binky wiped tears from her own eyes and moved closer to her brother. She snuffled, then sniffed, and sniffed again. "P—ewww! You stink!"

Egg's cheeks turned pink.

"Egg McNaughton, you need a bath!"

"I think that guy spilled some liquor on me when he fell," Egg decided. "I can smell it myself."

"Get out of those dirty clothes," Peggy ordered. "I'll find some old stuff of my dad's you can wear home."

"Jennifer, there's bacon and eggs in the refrigerator. Why don't you start frying some. Egg needs a full meal. Come on, Egg. You can get cleaned up in the bathroom here."

The girls burst into a flurry of activity, glad they could do something after hearing such a story. Egg retreated to the bathroom to shower and put on the shirt and pants Peggy found for him.

Lexi thought if the situation hadn't been so serious, it would have been comical. She and her friends were alternately feeding and scolding poor Egg. It was difficult to be both furious and curious at the same time.

Egg was still devastated by his experience. Lexi could see it in the way he carried himself, in his tone of voice, in the way he ate the food—like it was a duty, not a pleasure.

"We have so much—" he kept saying as he looked at his plate, "—and those people have so little."

"We can't help them right now, Egg," Jennifer said, her practical streak coming through.

"I guess I was never really convinced there were homeless people in Cedar River." Egg stared blankly out the window. "But we're a small community—if we all work together, we could find homes and food for every one of those people! Wouldn't that be great?" He perked up for a moment, then wilted again like a deflated balloon. "But this is just Cedar River. There's a whole world out there full of homeless, hungry people."

Lexi noticed Egg was on the verge of tears again. "Remember the Thanksgiving concert, Egg?" she said softly. "We're collecting money and food for those people. That's a start."

"What good will that do for the people outside Cedar River, Lexi? Think about New York City, Miami, Los Angeles. There are thousands of homeless we can't touch. I feel like I should be doing something. But what can I do? I'm just a kid!"

"You know better than anyone that being young doesn't keep you from helping," Peggy reminded him.

"Remember the 'Clean Up Cedar River' campaign?" Lexi said. "And your own 'Brick in Every Toilet' project to save water? It seemed like an impossible project at the start, but once everyone's enthusiasm grew and we focused our energy, Cedar River became a beautiful place once again."

"If we can do that, Egg, we can do anything!" Binky enthused.

"But I'm just one person, and you're just one person. That's not enough."

"One person working with another person, and another and another—together, we can do a lot."

"Do you really think so?" Egg's spirits rose a little.

"I don't think so, I *know* so," Lexi assured him. "Already you're not alone. Binky, Jennifer, Peggy, and I will help you. And you know you can count on Todd, Matt, Anna Marie, and Ruth."

"I'll bet Tim Anders and Brian James would pitch in. They're good guys."

"Of course. And if the Hi-Fives think they're missing something, they'll jump in with both feet. They can be difficult, but they can also be good workers if they put their mind to it."

"Mrs. Waverly will help in any way she can. She's already said that," Jennifer added.

"Right! And Mrs. Waverly is a good friend of Will Adams. He'll have lots of ideas of how we can help.

Don't you see, Egg? If we put our heads together, we can come up with something."

Jennifer stood up, her hands on her hips. "I think we should talk to Will Adams at the mission ourselves."

"Maybe we could volunteer to do something there," Peggy suggested.

"Like cook and serve at the soup kitchen." Binky's eyes glinted with excitement. "I'm sure they could use the help."

"I read about a project in the paper. Some group was collecting used toys and repairing them for needy kids. They were going to give them away at Christmas. Wouldn't that be a great idea for us?"

"If we all looked in our attics, we'd probably have old toys of our own we could donate to the needy."

"Exactly!" Peggy snapped her fingers. "We could set aside one weekend to collect toys. We could have drop-off boxes at the malls and a telephone campaign. Then we could spend evenings and weekends painting, sewing, and repairing toys. We could make a lot of little kids happy at Christmas this year. There are so many things we could be doing; I think we should get started soon!"

Egg bounced out of his chair like a rubber ball. "You're absolutely right!" he announced. "I guess I got a little depressed because I was tired and hungry. Now that I know I've got my friends behind me, my mind is full of ideas."

He grabbed Binky by the hand. "Get dressed, Binky. We're going home." Then he looked at Jennifer, Lexi, and Peggy. "As soon as you are ready, come over to our house. We'll all go down to the mission and talk to Will Adams today!"

Chapter Nine

The mission was quiet when Egg and his friends arrived. Breakfast had been served and the long dining room tables had already been cleared. The fragrance of fresh coffee still lingered in the air. The sun streamed through the spotlessly clean windows and made pools of brightness on the well-worn wood floor.

"Good morning!" Will Adams greeted them. "What a pleasant and unexpected surprise." The smile lines around his eyes deepened. "Would you like something to drink? Milk, orange juice?"

"Nothing, thanks." Egg looked around. "Why is it so quiet in here? Where are all the people?"

"Even though it's Saturday, some of them have gone to work."

"Work? You mean the people here have jobs?"

Will laughed. "Several of them do."

"Then why do they have to live here?"

"Most of those who are staying at the mission right now hold minimum-wage jobs. They simply don't earn enough to cover both rent and food—especially those who have children. As a stopgap measure, they are living at the mission until they can get on their feet.

"We help the people who stay here to set goals, like saving enough money to pay for an apartment for six months in advance. Achieving these goals helps them get ahead a little so they won't find themselves in the same predicament they were in the first time—having to choose between buying food and paying for the roof over their heads."

"Wow." Binky's eyes widened. "I sure have a lot to learn about this, don't I?"

Will was about to respond when the telephone rang. "Excuse me, I'll be right back. Why don't you wait in the lounge outside my office."

As Will disappeared inside, everyone sat down, and Egg gave another huge yawn. He'd been yawning all morning—and the frequency was increasing.

"Egg, you look like you need a bed," Jennifer observed.

"Yeah. I've been thinking about my firm mattress, clean sheets, and the warm, soft comforter on my bed." Usually Egg only looked this dreamy when describing food. "And my pillow. My perfect pillow that bends in just the right spot." Egg blinked twice as if coming back to reality from a daydream. "Last night I really didn't dare go to sleep. I thought I'd get mugged or something."

"It's the *or something* that scares me," Binky said frankly. "You risked your life, Egg McNaughton. I'm so mad at you I could just spit."

Egg looked away from his sister. "Oooh, I've never heard you talk like that before. You must really be mad."

"I am. I'm furious, Egg, and I'm scared." She looked around the room. "I'm seeing a side of life that I didn't even know existed. I don't like it. It frightens me. I've learned things I don't want to know about. I don't want to know that there are people without homes, without food and money. I don't want to know about people who are suffering."

"Why not, Binky, especially when they do exist?" Jennifer asked.

"Because then I feel like I have to do something about them!" Binky wailed. "It's just like the time the bathtub ran over and flooded through to the downstairs."

"Huh?" Egg and the others said in unison.

Binky looked a little sheepish. "Well, maybe it's a poor example, but one time I left water running in the tub while I was cleaning downstairs for Mom. Something got stuck in the overflow drain and water ran over the side and onto the floor. I was perfectly fine as long as I didn't know about the big mess upstairs. I was playing the radio, whistling, and doing my work. Then, all of a sudden, water started dripping through the ceiling, and I knew I had to go upstairs and find out what was wrong."

Binky drew in a deep breath. "Once I saw what was wrong, I knew that I had to clean it up. There was no one else home to help me."

"So?"

"Don't you see? By *knowing* that the bathtub had flooded over, I had to clean up the mess. As long as I didn't know there was trouble upstairs, I didn't have to do anything about it! It's the same way with poor people, isn't it? As long as we can ignore them and not know how they're suffering, it's easy not to pay attention and not to do anything to help them. But once you see them, *really see them*, like here, then you can't get them out of your mind anymore. You know in your heart that you should be doing something to help them."

"Well, Binky, that's the strangest analogy I've ever heard, but I think you're right," Jennifer agreed.

"Poor people and flooded bathrooms make me feel guilty." Binky sighed and sank deeper in the couch. "Isn't Will taking an awfully long time on the telephone?"

"He's a busy man, and he wasn't expecting us to come today."

"Yeah. You're right."

Jennifer and Peggy sat on chairs, and Lexi had joined Egg and Binky on the couch in the waiting room. They were all lost in their own thoughts when Jennifer broke the silence with a gasp. Angela Hardy and a woman who looked to be her mother walked out of Will's office.

Angela was dressed in her usual oversized white T-shirt and worn-out jeans. Her mother, who looked very much like Angela, and not much older except for deep worry lines around her eyes and mouth, wore much the same clothing, with a pale blue cardigan around her shoulders.

"Angela!" Egg was on his feet and moving toward the girl.

Angela's expression froze when she saw Egg and the girls.

"Angela? Do you know these young people?" Mrs. Hardy's voice was pleasant.

"Uh—"

"Hi. I'm Egg McNaughton." Egg thrust out a thin hand toward Mrs. Hardy. "We're classmates of Angela's."

"Friends from school. How nice. I haven't had the opportunity to meet any of Angela's classmates."

Lexi stood up. "My name is Lexi Leighton and this is Jennifer Golden, Peggy Madison, and Binky McNaughton, Egg's sister."

It was obvious that Angela's mother was happy to meet young people with whom her daughter went to school.

Angela, on the other hand, did not seem pleased to see them. Her step was hesitant as her mother drew her farther into the room.

"Angela told me she hadn't really met anyone at school yet. How nice to see you all."

"We came to see Will Adams," Lexi quickly explained.

"Will is helping our singing group plan a special Thanksgiving concert," Jennifer interjected. "He's a great guy."

Mrs. Hardy nodded in agreement. She was as friendly and open as Angela was closed and silent. Lexi could tell by the expression on Angela's face that she was mortified to be seen here by anyone from school.

"Will Adams is a very kind man," Mrs. Hardy said. "He's been especially good to Angela and me. I'll never be able to repay him. We've had some tough times, but Mr. Adams has hired me as his secretary." Mrs. Hardy smiled, and Lexi thought she was a beautiful woman.

"I have the best boss in the world. Of course, part-time work isn't really enough; I've been looking for a full-time job."

The more she spoke, the more Lexi liked Angela's mother. She was sweet and personable, but completely unaware of the fact that her daughter was shriveling up and dying right by her side.

Mrs. Hardy glanced at the clock on the wall. “I’d better get going. I need to do an inventory of food supplies in the kitchen this morning. Angela, why don’t you stay here and talk with your friends?” Without waiting for an answer, Angela’s mother patted her daughter on the arm and disappeared through the door that led to the kitchen.

It was obvious to Lexi that Angela did not want to visit with them, and there was an awkward silence until Egg broke the ice.

“Angela—we, uh . . .” Egg began.

Angela turned toward him, anger and fear written on her face. “What are you doing here?” she hissed.

“We came to talk to Will Adams,” Lexi reminded her.

“You? Friends of Will Adams? Why do I find that so hard to believe?”

“We met him through the school,” Peggy said gently. “Don’t you remember the day a busload of us came down here to visit?”

Angela’s eyes glazed over. “Oh. Yes, I remember.”

“The Emerald Tones and chorus Thanksgiving concert has been the talk of school for weeks,” Jennifer added.

Angela relaxed a little. “It’s just that I . . . well, I was surprised to see you all here when I walked through the door. It’s been hard for me to admit to anyone that I live down in this area. Does everyone at school know?”

Lexi glanced at Egg. He was squirming uncomfortably and she could almost read his mind. “No, uh

. . . we may be the only ones." Before Lexi could say any more, Egg began to speak.

"I'm really sorry, Angela. I feel like we're butting into your life. And we promise that we won't tell anyone that you're dependent on the mission for . . ."

"My mother works here!" Angela reminded Egg. She still clung to what shred of pride she had left. "You don't know anything about me, so don't try to apologize for my life."

"Maybe I know more about you than you think," Egg blurted.

Lexi wanted to clamp her hand over his mouth, but it was too late.

With his usual lack of forethought, Egg spilled out his entire story. He told Angela about the days he'd followed her. He admitted that after he'd discovered her secret he wondered what it would be like to be homeless. Then he told her what he'd done the night before.

"You what?" Angela's voice was angry and incredulous. "You assume that because you stayed out one night and slept on the street in a box that you know something about the homeless? What a joke. You rich kids don't even belong down here. We don't need your kind of help."

"But why? We want to help. Besides, you have nothing to be ashamed of." Egg tried to sound reassuring.

"Right! That's how much you know about it. Can you imagine what will happen to me when it gets around school that my mother and I live in a welfare hotel? That my mother works at the mission? I'll be the butt of everyone's jokes, that's what. And if they aren't joking behind my back they'll be staring at me. They'll know that I don't wear these tacky clothes because I want to, but because I have no choice."

"You're wrong about the kids at Cedar River High," Lexi said.

"Oh, really? I don't think so. I've been through this before. The last town we lived in gave us no peace. Once people found out about us, they laughed behind our backs. I'm just waiting for it to start all over again."

Lexi knew all Angela had left was her pride, and they'd unintentionally hurt that as well.

"Angela, we're sorry . . ." Jennifer began.

But the girl couldn't bear the conversation any longer and burst from the room, sobbing as she went.

All five sat in stunned silence for a moment.

"What have we done?" Binky murmured. "Have we really ruined her life?"

"I didn't mean for it to come to this . . . I didn't mean for this to happen," Egg repeated, with his head in his hands.

"I feel cheap," Jennifer groaned.

Peggy stood with tears running down her cheeks.

When Will Adams finally entered the room from his office, he took one look at the group and asked them to come inside and sit down. He closed the door, but it took some time before he could pry the entire story from them.

"Oh, Mr. Adams," Lexi cried. "Have we done something we can never undo?"

"I don't think so. But it may take some time to win back Angela's confidence."

"But none of us meant to hurt Angela."

"I know that. But Egg and Jennifer did infringe

on Angela's privacy. You can understand why she's so upset. Angela is a normal, proud teenager who hates what's happened to her and to her mother. She hates the stigma of poverty, just like any of you would in the same circumstances."

"I can't believe how awful I feel," Jennifer admitted.

"You're not the only one," Peggy said.

"The stupid part of this whole thing is that we came down here today to find out how to help the homeless," Jennifer explained, "but instead, we've practically ruined someone's life. How's that for bombing out?"

"Don't be too hard on yourselves," Will said, his smile returning. "I want you to know that if everyone in this country cared as much as you young people do, there wouldn't *be* a homeless problem. Put this behind you and move on. I appreciate the fact that you are caring and compassionate, and I believe that Angela, given time, will realize it, too."

"I don't think there's enough time in the world to get Angela to realize that and forgive us," Binky said mournfully. She wiped a tear from her cheek. "I know that Angela may never forgive us or speak to us again, but maybe there's some way we can do something to help someone else—you know, to pay for our stupidity."

"You have quite a way with words, Binky," Will chuckled. "There's no doubt that we can use lots of help here at the mission."

"We'll do anything," Egg offered.

"Anything at all," Lexi agreed.

"I'll scrub floors, wash windows," Jennifer added.

"I'll clean toilets!" Peggy blurted.

Will held up his hands. "Your enthusiasm is overwhelming, but I have something a little simpler and more pleasant that will help us a great deal. We're getting very short on the basics that we provide here at the mission. That's why I was so excited when Mrs. Waverly came to me with the idea of collecting money and food for Thanksgiving baskets. I think the project will make people in Cedar River aware of local needs and perhaps willing to donate more later. What I need is someone to head up a drive to collect things like blankets, socks, soap, toothpaste and toothbrushes, hairbrushes, combs—that kind of thing."

"You guys need toothbrushes?" Peggy gasped.

"A toothbrush is a pretty important item to someone who hasn't had one for a long time."

"Imagine not owning your own toothbrush!" Binky was appalled. The plight of the homeless was becoming more and more of a reality.

"That should be easy," Lexi said. "We have a friend whose mother works with several organizations. I'm sure Mrs. Winston could give us names and addresses of local groups. We could write letters or visit, asking for donations."

"Everybody has blankets they aren't using," Egg remarked.

"Soap, socks, and combs are pretty inexpensive items," Peggy said.

"It shouldn't be too difficult to get people to donate those things," Jennifer added.

"Replenishing our supplies would be a great help to us right now," Will said.

"I'd like to be in charge of this project," Egg offered. "I feel like I'm responsible for hurting Angela, and I should do something to make up for it."

"Egg, don't take all the blame. I didn't help matters," Jennifer admitted.

"Let him do it if he really wants to," Lexi advised. "He's a great organizer. Once he gets excited about something, you know he can't be stopped."

Binky rolled her eyes. "How well I know."

"Okay! Egg's in charge," Jennifer affirmed. "What do we do first?"

"I have an idea," Egg said, his eyes bright with enthusiasm. "We can announce the new drive at the Thanksgiving concert. By then the food and money will be collected and everyone will be aware of the needs of the homeless in our own hometown. We can tell everyone what we're going to be doing and announce a day for going house to house, business to business, asking for donations. I'm sure the editor of the *Daily News* would write an article about it."

"Maybe we could get other young people at church and school involved."

"We could go to every door in town."

"We could get enough toothbrushes and combs to last a lifetime!"

"This is the kind of enthusiasm I like to see," Will said happily. "In addition to your ideas, we can implement some of Pastor Lake's."

Lexi was immediately interested.

"He had a particularly good suggestion for the people who are staying here at the mission. While waiting for positions to open up in the job market, he suggested people living here create their own jobs."

"How can they do that?"

"Pastor Lake offered to announce at church that

people at the mission would be willing to do chores, such as mowing lawns and painting houses. Someone is always looking for a handyman to fix something around the house. The mission residents could put a percentage of their earnings into a kitty for advertising their services. Eventually, a handyman service might evolve into a real business. If nothing else, people will get to know others on an employee/employer basis. Who knows? They might find other jobs that way."

"Pastor Lake has some great ideas, doesn't he?" Binky said.

"He's a very compassionate and intelligent man," Will said. "He also suggested something else that I'm rather excited about."

"What's that?"

"Among the homeless in Cedar River, some are young children. Others are older, like Angela. Many mothers have left their homes because of abuse. Suddenly, the children no longer have a father's support, or a home to go to. Often they have had to leave behind prized possessions and favorite pets."

"Oh, how sad," Binky wailed.

"Pastor Lake is going to approach the board of his church about the possibility of forming a day-care center at the church for these homeless children. They would be cared for while their mothers work, and the older ones would have a place to come to after school for a snack, games, and a place to do their homework."

"Would there be many children to take advantage of it?" Peggy asked.

"Quite a few. My personal goal is to put myself out of business," Will said with a smile. "I'd like to find every homeless person in Cedar River a home, and every jobless person a job. Until that happens, however, we'll have to watch for those who still need our help."

"I want to help, but sometimes I think I'll never learn to mind my own business and not mess up so much," Egg moaned.

Will put an arm around Egg's shoulders. "Your intentions were good. That's the important thing. And now you are offering to head up a campaign to help the homeless. I think Angela will eventually understand that you didn't mean to hurt her."

"Do you honestly think so?"

"I'm positive. You've taken one of the hardest steps already."

"What's that?"

"Realizing that there *are* homeless people and being willing to do something about it."

"Thanks, Will. You've made me feel better already," Egg admitted. "But I'm still a little worried about Angela. Hurting her was the last thing I wanted to do. I'm crazy about her."

"Do you mind if I talk to her?" Will offered.

"You'd do that?"

"I'd be willing to try."

"Thanks. I'd really appreciate it."

Lexi stood, feeling they'd gotten the answers they'd come for. They all shook hands with Will and thanked him for his understanding and help.

Tonight, Will, Mrs. Hardy, Angela, and Egg would be in Lexi's prayers. They all needed God's help and direction.

Chapter Ten

"Leave your toothbrushes here, please. No, we can't take used ones. Combs and brushes there; socks over there. Blankets? Terrific. Put them in the big box at the end of the table."

Egg stood behind a long table in the school hallway. His arms and mouth were moving full speed, directing students who had brought donations for the mission. Egg had thrown himself wholeheartedly into the project. Each day during collection hours, he put on a green visor and a sweatshirt with *Give a Gift. You Can Afford It,* printed on it.

"Socks? Yes, we could use all sizes. And soap is another item we need lots of. Look in your bathroom closet at home. You're bound to have an extra bar."

Lexi and Todd covered their mouths and chuckled.

"He's really into this, isn't he?" Lexi remarked.

"I think he's even more enthused about this than he was about the 'Clean Up Cedar River' campaign."

"Egg is one of a kind." Lexi looked fondly at her lanky friend. He had half a dozen pens stuck in his pockets and one behind each ear. His Adam's apple bobbed as he spoke. Everything was under control—except maybe Egg.

"What do you think of my crazy brother?" Binky

came to stand beside Lexi.

"He's taking this awfully seriously."

"Yeah. I hope it lasts. And I hope Angela sees him working hard to help the homeless."

No one could deny that Egg was compassionate and enthusiastic when it came to helping those less fortunate than himself.

"Thanks to Egg, the drive to collect basic necessities for the mission has been more successful than any of us dreamed possible," Todd said. "He's made sure posters are up all over school, and he literally hounds people for donations."

"Right. As usual, Egg's gone a bit overboard," Binky said. "Last night, I heard him call Tim Anders at eleven o'clock to remind him to bring soap to school this morning."

"Mr. Adams will be ecstatic when he sees what's been collected so far."

"I'm sure he will." Binky looked at the rapidly growing piles. "Everything would be perfect if Angela would just come out of her shell."

Since they'd run into Angela at the mission, she'd become even more withdrawn. She never spoke to anyone at school, and never participated in class discussions. It was as though she were trying to make herself invisible, and Lexi thought she was doing a pretty good job of it.

Between classes Lexi, Todd, Binky, and Egg had permission to pack up the donations. After school they would be delivered to the mission.

"I can't believe all this stuff," Todd remarked.

Egg didn't say anything, but methodically began packing boxes.

"What's the matter, Egg?" Binky asked. "Don't

you think we got enough supplies today?"

"That's not it. I can't figure out why Angela won't speak to me. I feel like a real jerk."

"You're not a jerk, Egg. Angela's got to realize that we don't like her any less because she and her mother are living where they do."

"Maybe, but I still feel like I should make up for my blunders and the unhappiness I've caused. The trouble is, I don't know what to do." He packed toothbrushes as he spoke. "I can't feel good about helping others until I know that I haven't ruined Angela's life in the process."

"Where's Todd?" Lexi asked.

Jennifer, Peggy, and Binky joined her on the sidewalk after school.

"He's with Egg," Binky answered. "They're almost done loading boxes into the car. He said he'd pick us up."

"Are you sure there's going to be room?"

At that moment, Todd pulled up in his Ford coupe, Egg in the front seat beside him. "Looking for a ride?"

"Oooh, the backseat's full of boxes," Binky said. "Maybe we should walk."

"We'll make it. Pile in. Egg didn't pack the boxes in the backseat very tightly. I hate to admit it, but I wasn't any help loading the car."

"That's understandable, Todd. You're not supposed to be lifting anything," Lexi reminded him.

"Some days I think my football injury is just an excuse for being lazy," Todd said wearily. "I'm tired of babying myself."

"I'm not complaining," Egg said. "As long as I have a ride to the mission, I'm happy. Let's go. Will Adams is waiting for us."

"Drive fast," Binky ordered. She and Jennifer were crammed into the backseat with a stack of boxes.

"I can't go any faster than the speed limit," Todd reminded her. "If we get stopped, we won't get to the mission any sooner."

As they pulled up to the mission doorway, they saw several people leaning against the walls outside, smoking cigarettes or just visiting.

"It's a lot busier here now," Binky said. She peeked in to see that all the chairs inside were taken.

"That's because it's nearly suppertime." Jennifer inhaled deeply. "Can't you smell the food cooking?"

"Yeah. It must really smell great if you haven't had a hot meal yet today."

"I'm beginning to feel a little silly," Jennifer said. "Look at all the people milling around here. Are we suppose to carry these boxes past them while they stare at us?"

"It's not as if we're doing something wrong, Jennifer."

"I know, but it's kind of embarrassing anyway."

"It shouldn't be. We're trying to help."

"How about those people?" Jennifer whispered. "They must know we've collected this stuff for them."

"I suppose it's hard to take charity," Lexi admitted. "Especially if you've provided for your family in the past."

Just then Will emerged with a delighted grin on his face. "Hello! Welcome! Look at this car full of people and boxes!"

"Wait until you see the trunk," Todd said. "We're

going to need help getting this stuff inside."

"There are plenty of us here to do that. Just open the trunk and let us at it." With a wave of his hand, Will recruited a few of the men who had been watching with interest. "Help me carry these things to my office," he asked. In a matter of minutes, the car and the trunk were both empty.

"That was easy," Egg said. "It was a lot harder to pack the car."

"Many hands make light work," Will said. "Everyone is grateful for what you young people have done. By the look of it, you've completely replenished our supplies. Every time anyone uses something you've brought, they'll be thankful for your generosity."

"I wish we could do more," Egg said humbly.

Will looked at Egg with a sly smile on his face. "By the way, don't go yet. There's someone in my office who wants to talk to all of you."

"To us?" Egg looked surprised. "About what?"

"You'll see. Follow me."

"All of us?" Peggy asked.

Will nodded and led the way through the foyer and down the hall to his office. They entered the first door where the boxes they'd brought were stacked beside his secretary's desk. Then they walked into his private office.

Inside, a girl stood at the window, her back to them. Slowly she turned to face them in the dimming light.

"Angela?" Egg gasped. "You wanted to talk to us?"

"I think I'll see how things are going in the kitchen," Will said as he backed out the door, closing it behind him.

"My mother's working on the evening meal," Angela said. "Will's been great about helping her." Lexi could see the pride in her expression when Angela spoke of her mother. "Mom's an ambitious person. She's never been afraid of hard work."

Angela propped herself against the ledge of the window. "She blames our problems on the fact that she dropped out of high school in her junior year to have me. Of course she planned to go back and finish, but it was just too difficult after I was born.

"If she'd had a high-school diploma she could have gotten better jobs. Now she's working on her high-school equivalency." Angela smiled proudly. "Then she'd like to go on to college and major in education. She wants to be a teacher."

"That's impressive," Todd said.

"I know. She gets tired sometimes, working during the day and studying at night." Angela shook her head. "It's sure a lot easier to graduate from high school when you're a teenager."

Everyone was quiet, not wanting to discourage Angela's willingness to open up to them.

Angela turned to look out the window again. "I don't want to ever go through what my mother did. I want to finish high school and go to college. I want to *be* somebody, make something of myself."

Lexi was amazed at how different Angela seemed. Her anger was gone, and she was calm and thoughtful. She appeared to have accepted the fact that they all knew where she lived and why.

Her eyes brimmed with tears as she turned to Egg. "I was really shook—absolutely terrified—to discover I'd been found out. I imagined the awful things that might happen—people laughing, talking about me behind my back, avoiding me. But you guys are different."

"Why wouldn't you let us be your friends?" Binky asked.

"Because that way I didn't have any friends to lose. It's happened so many times before, and I never want it to happen again."

"Have you decided to trust us now?" Jennifer asked.

Angela nodded. "Every day since you saw me here at the mission, I've been waiting to hear the flak at school, but no one has said a thing. I finally realized that none of you had told anyone. You kept your word; my secret is still a secret. I can't tell you how much I appreciate that." Angela's voice quivered with emotion. "I hardly even know you, and you're the best friends I've ever had."

Egg looked close to tears.

"I also appreciate what you've done for the mission. Every day I've watched you collect the stuff you brought here today. You've thrown yourselves into this. A few years ago, I might have thought it was silly—but now I know how important it is.

"I remember the day Will gave me a new toothbrush. It hurt to know I didn't have anything to donate; that I'd be on the receiving end of your gifts."

"That's okay, Angela," Binky encouraged. "You'll give when you can."

Angela smiled. "I've never met teenagers who try so hard or want to help so badly. You guys are different. I don't know what it is, but you're special. You have something unique in your lives that others don't."

Lexi knew what it was. Christ was their Savior.

They were acting on His instructions from Matthew 25: "I was hungry, and you gave me food. . . ." Someday Lexi hoped to have a chance to explain that to Angela.

"I have something to ask you," Angela spoke again. "I'd really like all of you to give me another chance. I'm sorry for the way I've acted. I was wrong."

"Of course we'll give you another chance," Egg answered, almost too eagerly.

Binky jumped to her feet and enclosed Angela in a warm embrace.

The others hovered in a semi-circle around Angela, and overwhelmed her with their willingness to be friends.

There was a knock at the door. Will Adams stepped inside. "Supper is being served. Can you join us?"

Lexi spoke for the others. "Thanks, but it's time for us to go. Our parents will be wondering what happened to us. We'll talk another time, Angela. Maybe you could come over after school someday."

Angela nodded and smiled as the gang left the room, and she and Will joined the others in the dining room.

"Thanks again for all you've done," Will said.

"Anytime," Egg answered.

As they passed the tables full of people, who laughed and carried on animated conversation as they ate, Todd remarked, "They really don't look much different from our families, do they?"

"I guess I never really thought about it," Binky murmured, "but the homeless are people just like us."

Chapter Eleven

Egg pulled out his notebook and pen at the lunch table. At the top of a page he'd lettered: *Things We Can Do to Help the Homeless*. Beneath it, he'd numbered one through twenty.

"Okay, I'm ready for suggestions."

Binky shook her head and turned to Angela, who had joined them. "Sorry, Angela, but as you may have discovered, my brother gets a little tiresome at times. He has a one-track mind."

Angela laughed and looked at Egg with shining eyes. "I don't mind. I think he's cute."

Matt gave a loud hoot and slapped his hands on the table, until plates and silverware clattered. "Hear that, Egg? She thinks you're cute!"

"Oooo, I smell romance in the air," Jennifer teased.

Peggy and Lexi softly hummed the old Elvis tune, "Love Me Tender."

Angela giggled, and Egg blushed. Angela's statement was not a surprise to anyone. She and Egg had been looking at each other with love-sick eyes for the past several days.

"I've got an idea," Lexi said, diverting everyone's attention to the subject at hand. "We could talk to all the churches in Cedar River. If everyone worked together, we could get a lot more done. I'm sure Pastor Lake would help us with the contacts, don't you think?"

"Yeah," Egg agreed, and wrote down Lexi's idea.

"Maybe those with cars could volunteer to drive the homeless to job interviews," Todd suggested.

"Hey, that's a good one," Angela said. "My mom hated to spend busfare for job interviews, but she couldn't very well walk to every interview either."

"How many homeless kids are there in Cedar River?" Binky asked.

"Not too many," Angela said. "But across the country there are lots of kids without homes."

"Maybe we could write letters to the missions and shelters," Binky suggested. "We could send stories to the kids with a stick of gum or a quarter."

"Good idea, Binky." Egg wrote it down. "Definitely worth looking into."

"My mom used to be a teacher," Peggy began. "She says it would be nice if teachers volunteered to help with reading skills or studying for high-school equivalency tests at the mission."

"That is a tremendous idea!" Egg enthused, scribbling it down on the list.

"I still like our idea of collecting and repairing toys to be given to kids at Christmas," Binky reminded everyone. "We haven't done anything about it yet."

"I have," Todd interjected. "I asked my brother Mike if we could use the storeroom at his garage to collect and repair toys. He said that would be fine."

"That's a start," Egg said. "What are we waiting for?"

"We could have Mrs. Waverly announce at the concert what we're doing. People could bring toys to the garage or the school," Todd said. "Let's meet at Mike's garage tomorrow after school with whatever we can come up with by then, and get started."

Suddenly Egg was on his feet snapping his fingers. "I've got it!" he shouted. "It's the best idea yet!"

"Tell us, Egg," Binky ordered. "You look like a clown on a pogo stick."

"I can't. I have to talk to Mrs. Waverly first." He dashed out of the room, leaving everyone puzzled.

"What's his problem?" Peggy wondered.

Lexi summed it up for all of them. "With Egg, who can tell?"

It was finally time for the Thanksgiving concert, and the gymnasium was filling up fast. Binky peeked through the curtains every so often, and each time came away a little more pale and excited than the last. "Do you know how many people are out there?" she gasped.

Finally Mrs. Waverly asked her not to peek through the curtains anymore. She was making herself and everyone else nervous.

The Emerald Tones and the school chorus were warming up. Lexi had butterflies in her stomach and a knot in her throat.

"Stage fright?" Todd teased as he took her hand.

"Stage *terror* is more like it," Lexi retorted. "I can't remember ever being this nervous before a concert."

"You'll do fine. We've certainly rehearsed enough." Todd looked particularly handsome in his

Emerald Tones jacket and dark pants. His shoes were polished, and he had a fresh haircut.

"You look great tonight," Lexi told him.

Todd put his arm around her waist and gave her a squeeze. "You look great yourself."

"We all look nice." Jennifer twirled on tiptoe. "We're going to knock their socks off with this concert."

"Places. Places. Places, everyone." Mrs. Waverly scurried around like a mother hen gathering her chicks. When her back was turned, Binky took one more peek through the split in the curtain and nearly fainted dead away.

"It's completely full out there!" she gasped. She flapped her arms and jumped up and down. "It's going to be standing room only! Can you believe it? They've taken down all the bleachers and the floor is full of chairs." She grabbed her stomach. "Oh, I'm so nervous I think I'm going to throw up."

"That will certainly be a help," Jennifer commented sarcastically.

"And guess who I saw sitting near the front?" Binky said. Before anyone could guess she answered her own question. "Angela and her mother."

"Super!"

"I'm so glad they could come."

"We'll all sing our best just thinking about Angela."

"Line up, people. Please!" Mrs. Waverly's hair was neatly piled on top of her head, without the characteristic pencils, and she looked particularly attractive in a navy blue suit with a lacy white blouse.

Sometimes, Lexi mused, it was hard to remember that teachers were people too, with lives and families of their own. Tonight Mrs. Waverly's husband was sitting in the front row. That firmed her resolve to sing her best.

"Where's Egg?" Binky asked. She peered to the right and to the left. "He's supposed to be here."

"He's wandering around somewhere in a cloud," Jennifer said with a dismissing wave of her hand. "You know Egg."

"Yes, I know my brother well. Something is up. He'd be right here if he weren't fooling around, getting into some kind of hot water."

"Don't be so suspicious, Bink," Jennifer said, trying to calm her.

Binky's eyes darted back and forth. "Oh, what is it? I know he's up to something. I just don't know what it is . . . yet."

At that moment, Egg came skidding onto the stage and took his place. There was no time to ask him where he'd been or what he'd been doing because the curtain shuddered and began to rise. The concert was about to begin.

Lexi couldn't remember the Emerald Tones or the chorus ever sounding better. Every voice seemed in perfect pitch. The roar of the crowd at the close of their final number told her that the audience agreed.

They had prepared an encore in the event of such a response. Lexi held her hands to her stomach and waited for their cue to begin. But to her surprise, Mrs. Waverly held up a hand to quiet the crowd. Mrs. Waverly hadn't told them she would speak to the audience before the encore!

"I'd like your attention for a moment, please. I would like to introduce to you someone with a very important message. Ladies and gentlemen, Mr. Edward McNaughton." Mrs. Waverly turned and offered the microphone to Egg.

"Egg!" Binky whispered. "What's he doing? I *knew* something was up. I just knew it."

Egg stepped forward to stand behind the microphone.

"I know that every one of you here tonight has heard about our drive for food and money to provide boxes for the needy this Thanksgiving. Many have also had the opportunity to hear about our necessities drive for the mission. We want to thank you for your cooperation and generous support of these projects.

"Tonight, I have another project to announce. I'm sure some of you may feel you've given enough. But please, just for a moment, put yourself in a different place and time—a time when you were less comfortable than you are today, when all the things you have today were just a dream. Pretend with me for a moment that you don't have a home; that you don't have a job; that you don't have an income; that every meal you eat might be your last because you don't know where the next is coming from.

"Picture for a moment that tonight when you leave the high school gymnasium you don't have a place to go. There's no car, no warm garage, no cozy home, no comfortable bed waiting for you. Then realize that there are thousands of people in this country today in that very situation.

"They have no home other than a shelter, a mission, or perhaps a cardboard appliance box over a city grate. Their dinner plans include going to a mission to stand in line and hoping that the meals don't run out, or searching garbage cans for discarded bits of food."

Egg paused and looked out over the packed gymnasium. "Until Mrs. Waverly suggested giving a Thanksgiving concert to benefit the needy, I'd assumed that everyone had things at least as good as I did. Not so. My eyes were opened even more when I met Mr. Will Adams at the mission. He showed me how fortunate I really am. I have friends, family, a home, and all the food I need to eat. I began to think that I should use some of my good fortune to help others."

Egg's eyes glowed and he gestured expansively with his hands, totally immersed in his speech.

"I began to think about my own personal wealth. Wealth, you ask? What kind of wealth does that skinny kid up there have?" Egg smiled at the audience. "I have good health and energy, an allowance, and a family that supports me. I've begun to realize that I can use the things I have—my youthful energy, enthusiasm, and my allowance to help others who are less fortunate than I am."

Egg went on to tell the audience about the projects that the mission had undertaken and of those Pastor Lake was sponsoring. He spoke of Mike's willingness to allow them to use a storeroom in his garage to restore toys for children for Christmas.

"Homelessness is a *human* problem. That makes it *our* problem," Egg concluded. "The next time you see a homeless person on the street, imagine yourself walking in his or her shoes. Imagine what it would be like to be afraid, ashamed, and without resources. Then realize that the blessings God has given you are meant to be shared."

When Egg was finished speaking, Lexi doubted there was a dry eye in the entire gymnasium.

Egg pointed to Brian James and Tim Anders who stood at the back doors with baskets in hand to collect the donations. Then Egg bowed his head and stepped away from the microphone as Mrs. Waverly led the choir in a final hymn of thanksgiving. Without encouragement, the audience joined in, tears streaming from many eyes, including Lexi's.

Chapter Twelve

"More stuffing?" Ben moved from table to table carrying a serving bowl piled high with bread and mushroom dressing.

Lexi walked behind him with mounds of fluffy white potatoes and giblet gravy.

Mrs. Leighton passed cranberries and olives, while Mr. Leighton carved the huge turkey. Lexi's dad looked up and winked at her over the heads of those seated at the long tables in the mission dining room.

"This is fun, Lexi!" Ben said enthusiastically. "I like being here for Thanksgiving."

Lexi had to agree. Her family had come to help her friends serve the Thanksgiving meal. The long tables were covered with white tablecloths and decorated with orange and yellow streamers and fat paper turkeys for centerpieces. Thanksgiving hymns played in the background and everyone was in a festive mood.

"There's plenty of corn and green beans. Would you like some more?" Egg was in charge of vegetables.

Binky was doling out hot rolls and butter while Peggy, Jennifer, and some of the others were in the kitchen cutting pumpkin pies for dessert.

Even Will Adams was at the table being served. *It feels right,* Lexi mused, *to be serving these people.* It felt better to be giving instead of receiving; sharing instead of hoarding; serving instead of being served. It reminded Lexi of Jesus at the Last Supper when He'd humbled himself and washed the disciples' feet.

Todd's parents had also come to help. After they'd eaten, Mrs. Winston had plunged up to her elbows in soapy water washing dishes, while Mr. Winston dried them.

Angela was pouring coffee. As Lexi walked by her, she teased good-naturedly, "Don't spill!"

Angela looked up and grinned. "Don't worry. I don't want to do anything to ruin this perfect day."

Having Angela serving with us does make the day perfect, Lexi thought. Angela was unbelievably generous, giving of herself without regard to her own needs.

Every dinner guest seemed grateful, and most expressed their deep appreciation. Lexi felt like she should be thanking *them.* It was a privilege just to be there! Her whole outlook had changed; she saw people through new eyes. Never before had she felt so closely linked to complete strangers.

As the dining room gradually emptied and people said their thanks and goodbyes, those that had served joined the others in cleaning up the kitchen. When the last dish was dried and the last pan put away, the Winstons and Leightons joined Lexi's friends around a table in the center of the room. Angela and Egg served them pumpkin pie and coffee.

All agreed that preparing and serving the Thanksgiving dinner here was a very rewarding experience, one that they would like to repeat.

When the adults and Ben had left, Lexi and her friends stayed to visit with Angela.

"I should be going home," Jennifer said with a sigh. "It was a wonderful Thanksgiving."

"Better than I ever expected," Peggy admitted.

"Before you all go, maybe you'd like to see where I live," Angela said unexpectedly. "My mom would like to get to know you better."

"Sure," Lexi said. She'd never thought Angela would actually invite them to the hotel where she and her mother lived.

They left the mission through a side door and crossed the alley behind it. The name printed in a half circle above the hotel door was barely legible: The Prince Hotel.

"The Prince is a welfare hotel, as you all know," Angela explained. "It's handy for us, because it's so close to the mission where Mom works and we have two meals a day. It's hard to cook in our room, because there's no kitchen, just a hotplate."

She led them upstairs and down a long hallway to a twelve-by-twelve-foot room. The furnishings were sparse, but the room was clean and bright, with fresh curtains at the windows. The two single beds were made up neatly with a thin blanket on each. A ragged teddy bear sat on the pillow of Angela's bed.

On the bureau were a few pictures. "That's my dad." Angela pointed to a handsome youth. "Mom doesn't like to have the picture out, but I do. It reminds me of happier days."

"Did you have a dog?" Binky asked, pointing to a picture of a small white poodle.

"That's Frenchy." Angela looked suddenly sad.

"We had to leave him when we came here. I hope someone's taking good care of him."

Angela's mother quietly joined them. "I'm glad you could come up and see where we live. It isn't much, but it's home for now. That was a delicious dinner you served today."

Before anyone could respond, Mrs. Hardy continued, "I want to thank all of you for everything you've done for Angela; for befriending her and treating her as an equal. You're the nicest bunch of kids I've ever met."

Lexi nodded shyly. "We're learning anyway. Angela's helped us to be aware of those around us, taught us to reach out to those beyond our own little group."

"There's always a lot to learn," Mrs. Hardy said. "But everyone isn't as willing as you young people have been. Thinking about the homeless and those less fortunate isn't pleasant. Denying that such people exist is much easier than finding ways to help them. I know that's how I was.

"I never believed I'd find myself in this situation. All I ever really wanted was a safe place for myself and my child. My husband and I were together a very short time. We were young and inexperienced, and had a lot of responsibility on our shoulders before we were ready for it. I lived with a lot of fear and worry after he left us. I was terrified of not being able to take care of Angela."

Egg shifted awkwardly on his chair and tears welled up in his eyes. "I suppose we'd better be going," he said. "Our parents are expecting us at home. My grandparents are visiting this evening. I was wondering, uh . . ."

"Yes, Egg?"

"Uh, well, uh . . . would it be all right if Angela came home with me to meet my grandparents?"

Angela blushed and turned to her mother for an answer.

Mrs. Hardy smiled. "Why Egg, I think that would be fine. Just bring her back by ten."

Now Egg was blushing, too. "No problem. Thanks, Mrs. Hardy. You have a nice place here . . . uh, see you around."

When the others had said goodbye to Angela's mother, they all hurried downstairs behind Egg and Angela.

Outside, Binky flung her arms in the air and danced around until she staggered with dizziness.

"What are you doing?" Jennifer asked.

"I just feel so good. So free . . . so thankful. I have great friends, good parents, a home. I'm even thankful for my brother Egg."

"All right! I'm the best thing you've got going for you, Binky McNaughton."

"Well, I don't know about that! You can be a big pain in the neck, you know. But lately, you've been all right."

"Get in the car," Todd ordered. "I'm going to drive you home as fast as I can before either of you forgets how thankful you are to have each other."

After dropping off Angela, Egg, and Binky at the McNaughtons', Todd took Jennifer and Peggy home. When he and Lexi arrived at her house, Todd's parents' car was parked in the driveway.

"It looks like my folks stopped here for coffee."

"Come on in, then," Lexi offered.

The Winstons and Leightons were still at the

kitchen table, while Ben was busy coloring at the counter.

"We owe a big thank you to you kids for this day," Dr. Leighton said. "It was one of the most enjoyable Thanksgivings I've ever experienced."

"I agree," said Mrs. Winston. "For once I felt like we fulfilled the real purpose of the holiday."

"It *was* great, wasn't it?" Lexi sank happily into a chair.

"Oh, by the way, Lexi," Dr. Leighton said. "Your friend Will Adams approached me about hiring Mrs. Hardy at the veterinary clinic on a part-time basis. I told him you were my help, but I'd talk to you about it. I know how busy you are during the school year. If it's all right with you, Mrs. Hardy could be my regular help, and you could come in whenever you felt you had the spare time."

"That would be great, Dad! It would take the pressure off when I'm bogged down with studies. Angela says her mom's a real good worker too."

"I'm sure she is. Will thought that if she could work at my clinic during the school year, she'd be ready to take her high-school equivalency test in the spring. Then she could look for another job while you worked during the summer months. How does that sound?"

"It sounds perfect. Absolutely perfect. I really have been awfully busy. And it would be a great opportunity for Angela's mom."

Lexi threw her arms around Todd's neck and twirled with him around the room. "Everything's working out, Todd. Can you believe it? It's a miracle. I've never had so much to be thankful for in my whole life."

Lexi couldn't be happier. This was a Thanksgiving she would remember for the rest of her life.

BOOK #18

Lexi's friend Ashleigh comes to visit, but there's something different about her. Can Lexi's friends accept it? Find out in Cedar River Daydreams' *More Than Friends*.

A Note From Judy

I'm glad you're reading *Cedar River Daydreams*! I hope I've given you something to think about as well as a story to entertain you. If you feel you have any of the problems that Lexi and her friends experience, I encourage you to talk with your parents, a pastor, or a trusted adult friend. There are many people who care about you!

I love to hear from my readers, so if you'd like to receive my newsletter and a bookmark, please send a self-addressed, stamped envelope to:

Judy Baer
Bethany House Publishers
6820 Auto Club Road
Minneapolis, MN 55438